THE TALE OF A MASSACRE

2020 WASN'T JUST ABOUT THE PANDEMIC

V V S KRISHNA ADITYA

Made with ♥ on the Notion Press Platform
www.notionpress.com

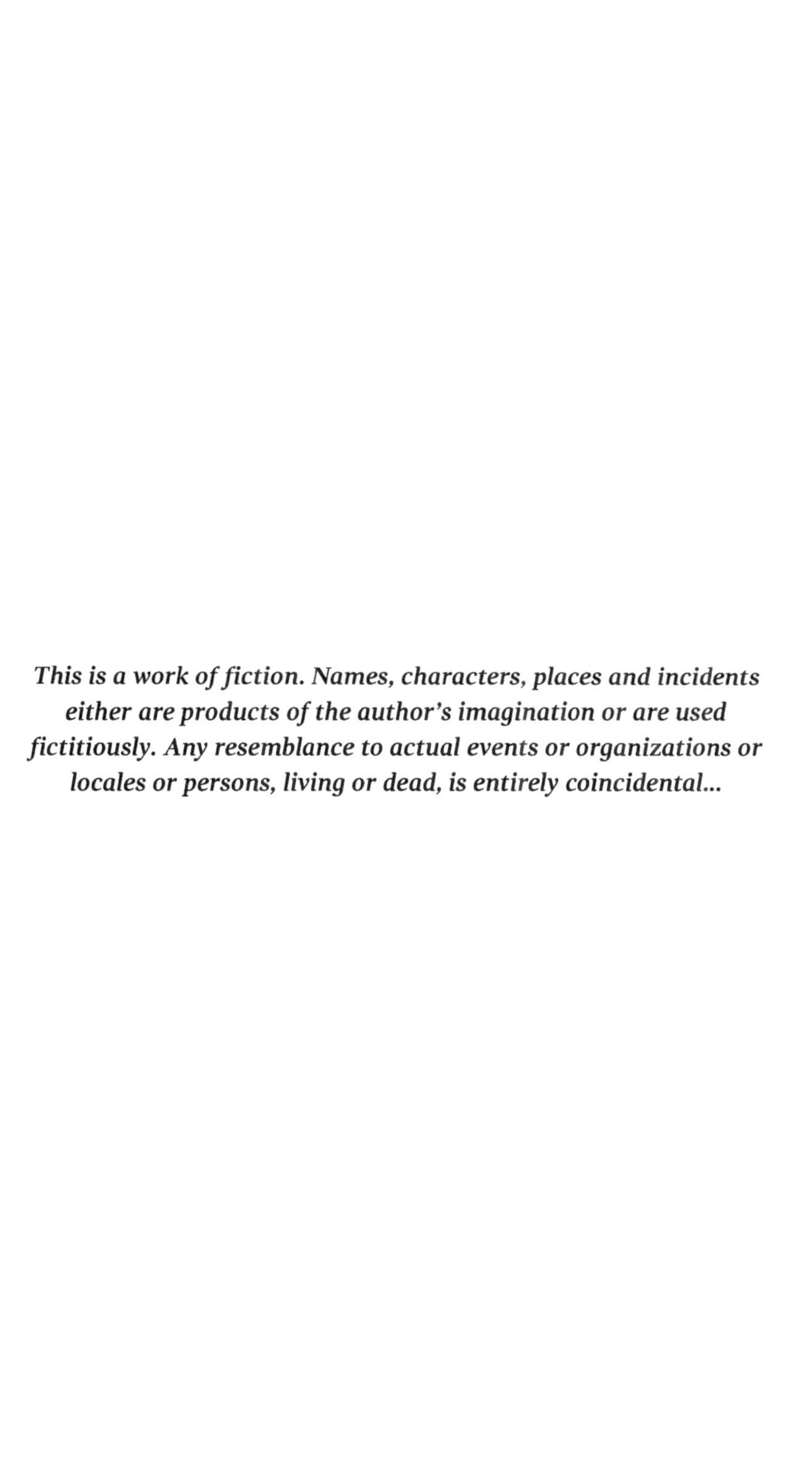

This is a work of fiction. Names, characters, places and incidents either are products of the author's imagination or are used fictitiously. Any resemblance to actual events or organizations or locales or persons, living or dead, is entirely coincidental...

Contents

Foreword

It is a true honor that the opportunity to write these words has been presented to me, especially as an avid reader myself and as a true supporter of quality content. Since 2002, precisely from the day I was born, I have had the pleasure of knowing Aditya VVSK as he is my cousin brother. Destiny installed us as default, unmodifiable settings in each other's lives, so I guess I actually did not have much of a choice and neither did he, but I am more than glad that destiny did its work the way it did. Our relationship has progressed from being distantly acquainted cousins to becoming best friends who know everything about one another. Regardless of the fact that we have lived on opposite sides of the world all our lives (and continue to do so), with me living in the United States and him in India, I have watched him grow from being a small kid to now being a writer with immense literal intellect. Aditya is one of the most well-spoken and sensible individuals that I know; he is keen and aware on how to react and adapt to different situations in a sophisticated manner. His straightforwardness can be perceived as a bit much by others at times, but it is the quality that I appreciate and respect about him the most. I can always count on him to give me his raw, honest opinions and feelings about me or the given circumstances to keep me in check, which is rare to find in today's ambiguity-filled world. He is one of the very few people I reach out to whenever I feel the need to confer with someone, get advice, or just speak out to relieve the burden that is on my mind. He is also probably one of the most multi-talented people I have ever met in my life. It constantly surprises me how he manages to have a work-life balance all while doing so much with such consistency, dedication, and precision. The first work of his that I read was a short childhood inspired story which he recently developed into a podcast episode on Spotify. At that point in time, I realized that this guy has a talent with words, but it was when I read his first officially published book, *Sacred Beings*, that I recognized he can create works of art with his talent. From then onwards, he has been regularly sharing his various creative pieces of writing with me with each one depicting a whole new journey. Personally, I exhibit a love for the suspense thriller genre and a while back when Aditya told me that he was starting on a new concept of this genre, I was excited and intrigued to read what story he was going to serve fresh on the menu this time around. Little did I know then that the story he told me about at that point was going to be published as a novel and I would be writing the foreword for it. For starters, this particular book displays a variety of elements, ranging from on-edge, anticipative sequences to unexpected twists to high stake events. When I got the chance to read this story for the first time, Aditya sent it to me one chapter at a time and each time I finished one chapter, I could not wait for him to send the next one. I still remember he made me wait a whole day to read the last two chapters just to leave me on a cliffhanger, keep me hooked, and further build the suspense. For me, this novel is highlighted through the manner in which the story is narrated from different points of view, the timeline that of events that transpires, and the notable development of every character. Moreover, the story lays a strong initial foundation, and it then progresses on to establish an even stronger plot through the incorporation of background information, dialogue, flashback, escalating tension, and different levels of pacing within the story. While reading, the detailed insight that is provided about each character allows for the audience to form a personal connection with them and serves as a way to experience the story from their standpoints by being a part of their actions and thought processes, in addition to giving a multi-dimensional effect to the story itself. This is especially prominent given the fact that all of the characters have their own backstories and lifestyles, but they are each brought together under one common situation. To describe this in other words, the entire novel stems from the conflict which exists between the protagonists and the antagonist and how the group of protagonists go about approaching the problems caused by the antagonist. This book will give you the taste of a five-star level full-course meal, dessert included, with its action, suspense, emotions, and drama. Aditya VVSK wrote this story with the intention to not have his audience just plainly read the novel, but to indulge the readers in a roller coaster like experience; as far as my opinion goes, I believe that he crossed his t's, dotted his i's, and satisfied his intended purpose to the core. As I mentioned before, even though I am Aditya's cousin sister, I am a genuine supporter of content that projects high caliber and that is the true main reason as to why I did not think twice when he asked me if I could write this foreword for this novel. As you approach the following pages, you will come to understand each word that I have stated here in this foreword, so prepare yourself to dive in because you are about to go on a journey which is filled with ups and downs, twists and turns, and a story that will surely be etched in your heart for a long time.

Enjoy Yourself,
Saialekhya Vatturi

Preface

Finally it's here, "THE TALE OF MASSACRE".

From tearing plenty of pages, backspacing countless words, deleting 100s of word files, brainstorming for ideas, doing multiple research studies, and from hating my thoughts to drafting a proper book, which was beyond what I had in my mind. I was completely satisfied with it's output. It's been a long time since I wrote something of this kind. This was something I was looking forward to. A thirller filled with lot of violent episodes that made the plot bloodier.

2020 it was, don't remmber the exact date, the time when we were all busy playing ludos, ignoring the online classes, do nothing except eat, sleep. If you ask about how did you get the idea of the plot, even I don't have any answer. It was developed over time. My major inspiration for my book are the DC comics which includes one of my favorites "THE KILLING JOKE", the duels between Batman and Joker, the scenes between them, those dialogues, the confrontations, they were my true driving force to write something of this kind. Crime is always my personal favorite always came up with short stories but not a fully planned crime thriller like this. It took like almost 3 years to complete this. I can't reveal much about the book in its preface itself. So all I have to say is there will be a set of people who like it and few who don't and I respect your opinions and take your inputs for my further improvement. I personally thank all the buyers and I hope I won't dissapoint you all.

Instagram : @mr_vvsk_

e-mail : vvskaditya@gmail.com

• • •

Happy Reading!

CHAPTER I

The Nation wants to Know

They are many black days in the Indian History, starting from the Jallianwala Bagh massacre to 26/11 Mumbai attacks. Today's date is going to be added to that list, "28th October 2030". The head of democratic India- The President, went missing. The country is on high alert. Panic rose, questions have been raised on security, and the opposition party of the country started their war of words against the ruling party. Social media trolls on the President started becoming viral and the fourth pillar of democracy started framing their own theories and suddenly the foreign media started focusing on the missing president. Prime Minister has called for the press meet immediately after returning to Delhi from Mumbai after hearing the big news. What answers will the Prime Minister now give to the press and the citizens of the country and not only the citizens of our country but the whole world is now in a huge question.

Prime Minister "Good evening, everyone, this evening isn't that good but we are trying to make it. I was in Mumbai as a part of my election campaign and then suddenly I got a call from President's chief security officer who informed me about the missing president and I was shocked just like y'all, after hearing the news about our President who went missing after his return from Russia. I appointed the best men to do this job and I assure you that we are going to find the President as soon as possible. I request the opposition to postpone the elections since the country is now without the President and I informed the election commission as well. So, no elections or campaigns until we find the President. Our priority will be finding the President". One of the press member raises a question, "Sir, now the President went missing who are we expecting to be in that position for now". Prime Minister "Vice President obviously, temporarily until we find the President". Press

"Sir how can we expect the common people to be safe when the President with high security went missing". Prime Minister "The security forces are trying their best to reduce the crime in our country and fortunately the crime rate in our country is reducing but this one was something unexpected and behalf of all the security forces I apologize to all the citizens of my country". Press "Is this just a beginning like something bigger which happened in 2020 Hyderabad". Prime Minister "We can't conclude that soon but we are prepared". Press "Any details about who is handling this case?". Prime Minister "The I.I.A. along with other security forces like RAW, army, etc. And thank you for coming I have to leave because the President went missing and I have to speak with other people as well. Jai Hind'. Prime Minister watching the news in his car on the way to his office, the opposition party leaders in the channel "The Prime Minister is scared about the result of elections that's the reason he postponed it. The president's kidnap is all a well-planned drama". Prime Minister with low voice "Idiots".

The broadcast started on the news channels. Reporters "**The nation wants to know**". Prime Minister has called a meeting with all the heads of the I.I.A., other agencies, the army, the SP of Delhi, the Home Minister, and the defence minister. Prime Minister "You guys have a big task ahead. Every move we take raises questions and controversies but we have to do anything to bring back our President. So, any updates so far?". I.IA head Krishna Chaitanya "Sir, so far what we have is just the beginning of the story. The President left Russia on 27th October 2030 at 7 PM IST. He landed in Delhi at 2 AM IST and then his car started at 2:30 AM, it reached the Rashtrapati Bhavan at 3:13 AM but he didn't make it. All the CC cameras were checked everything was clear except the Sardar Patel Marg. The officers who were escorting him informed him that the path was dark and with smog due to Diwali celebrations. So, we assume that his car went missing somewhere on Sardar Patel Marg. We got no clue, the person behind this planned it very well, and he gave us nothing, it's a clean crime without any black spots or holes. But we hope that we can find something so that we get a big breakthrough and solve this case. It's tough but really important as well. Every detail counts, every clue matters, we don't neglect anything". Prime Minister "Any idea who?". Krishna Chaitanya "Our country has many enemies inside and outside our border. Could be anyone from terrorist organizations, Naxals, Anti-Nationals, or enemy countries, we can't come to any conclusion with very less information, to be frank, no information but we are trying our level best to get our president back". Prime Minister "I can understand the situation but we have to act quick, no choice left. You have to do your best". Krishna Chaitanya "On it sir Jai Hind".

Krishna Chaitanya reached the I.I.A. head office and gathered his best men and started his work with 3 teams. Meanwhile, senior officer Nandini entered his cabin. Nandini "Hello KC can I get 10 min, really important". KC “more important than the missing president?". Nandini "About that". KC "Sure sit, what brings you here". Nandini "A plan". Kc "go on". Nandini "I know you guys are very busy with your plans but I have a complete team of 5 who are extremely great with their work. They are excellent in their fields and I believe they can handle this well". KC "And I believe in you, tell me about them". Nandini "I got a good hacker, a tech genius, a strong man with good accuracy in shooting and...". KC with an irritated face "and I got people 2 hands and 2 legs who are searching to find some or the other clue since morning and the Media is literally dancing on my head and I am getting calls directly from Prime Minister as if I am his newly married wife, hello honey where is the President, (shouts) no secrets give me the names". Random person opens the door "Sir all okay". KC "the president is been missing since morning, go and find him and don't enter my cabin till you get him". Nandini "Cool... breath in breath out I haven't seen you this angry since.". KC "2020". Nandini "Yes 2020". KC "Ohk names?". Nandini "Anupam, Akanksha, Bhargav, Chakit, and Dinesh". KC calms himself and "huh... seriously? Team 2020, whatever I am not gonna trust these guys again and I am not going to repeat the same mistake. Don't take me back to mission failure 2020. Please you may leave. I am really busy right now". Nandini

"Trust me this time it is going to work". KC "Its a failed mission, and I am not going to include a failed team to fail me again". Nandini in anger, "Don't say it again or else I am goanna smash your head like a golf ball. You and I both know that they were the people who had put an end to it. In records, you all labelled it as a failed mission but deep inside you know they saved the city from the upcoming threats. The city now we see is because of them. Trust me I will not let you down this time, they deserve a second chance". KC in low voice "I know but the Prime Minister is not going to allow the people from a failed mission. He recommended me few officers and I appointed another few who are the best in our department, we have sufficient masterminds to lead the mission, and if necessary, I will contact you, I know you came this far with huge expectations but I am so sorry to disappoint you". The same random person "I heard someone shouting, all, okay?". KC "I told you to open the door only when you find him". Random person "Find whom". Nandini laughs and KC in anger "The President, you idiot gets out now". Nandini "Brilliant officers appointed". KC "do you still have their contacts?". Nandini "is it a 'yes'?". KC "it is and not, fine you lead the operation along with your team secretly as our Plan B. I can give you the minimal resources possible but careful and last, I am not involved in this and you have to take complete responsibility for the team and its result". Nandini "Thank you so much KC". KC "I believe in second chances, go on I trust you but promise me you will get him". Nandini "Get whom" laughs. KC "come on". Nandini "By the way Harika called you twice. All the best after going home". KC "hope you guys don't find the president and I stay here for years".

The news of the missing president has spread like a wildfire. The no. of teams working on this case is officially 3 and unofficially one- Nandini's team 2020. It's been 10 hours since the President went missing. Nandini is now on a mini mission to get her team together. Mini mission no. 1, get Anupam. Anupam is an awesome techie, his hands work very fast, and was a brilliant hacker and worked on a few secret missions for IIA He resigned from his job in 2020 and then joined Infosys as a software developer.

Infosys Delhi branch. The branch head of the company called Anupam to come to his cabin. Anupam wondering why, goes to his cabin, and to his surprise he sees Nandini. Branch head "Have a seat, Anupam, you guys talk I will be back in 10 min". Anupam "Hi ma'am". Nandini "Hi Anupam here take a seat". Anupam sits "It's been a long time since we met. I almost forgot you". Nandini "Really? Don't lie". Anupam "How can I forget that bloody year. Those deaths, the destruction, the collapse of the city which took years to recover, The failure of one of the best intelligence agencies in the world". Nandini "It was, it is, and always will be a nightmare to everyone who worked in that case. But I am not here to talk about that". Anupam "Then what?". Nandini "It's been almost a decade since we all met so why not have a reunion". Anupam "wait, I know where this is going, you want to involve me in some mission. Don't lie. Yes or no". Nandini "A little confidential but yes I am involving you in a mission to find the missing person". Anupam "No way, I have a family and a job and I can't leave them to join your mission. I got a life. What if something happens to me? Who will take the responsibility for my wife and children"? Nandini "You are a tech guy not the man with a gun, so chill. Nothing is going to happen to you". Anupam "I beg you please I don't want to get involved in any of this stuff". Nandini "This is just a missing case, no guns, no bombs, no deaths a simple missing case but the person missing is (pause) the president, that's it". Anupam in shock "what the f". Nandini "Just listen you have been given a second chance You can't erase or correct what happened in the past but now you can help us find the president and make this mission a success. Think about it. This office this paperwork, these projects are not you, the Anupam whom I knew was a guy with headphones and a weird notebook on his lap tying something, cracking lame jokes, and giving quick infos. Bring that Anupam back. Prove yourself to the people who said you are not fit for this department. Fine...it's up to you, I am leaving". Anupam "Hey wait, What's the process to join the I.I.A once you left it". Nandini "You are hired". Anupam "What about my job?". Nandini "You are a software developer in Infosys who applied leave for 3 months to have a reunion with your friends. Your job is in safe hands and here is your leave granted by your manager, this is your ticket to Kashmir, you will find Bhargav and Chakit there. Bring them to Delhi, you have 24 hours. The flight leaves in 45 mins. Rush now and show this letter if anyone stops you at the airport". Anupam "Yes ma'am". Anupam leaves for the airport and boards the flight and meanwhile Nandini boards another flight to Chennai.

Meanwhile, somewhere in India in a car with President tied in chains. The driver of the car "Careful with him we need that man". Other people in that car "We have to be more careful, the I.I.A. and everyone are looking for this man". A man with his left cheek burnt "He is just a pawn in my game, my plan is to get the king" laughs "The game just started". A song from a radio started to play and it goes like, "Jeena yahan marna yahan...".

CHAPTER II

Muscles and Brains

Narration: Anupam

Pine trees, snowfall, pleasant atmosphere, spicy food, and beautiful sceneries, if there is a heaven on this Earth then it is here, the crown of India, the paradise of nature 'Kashmir'. But not as beautiful as we think, the place where there lies unity there also lies anti-nationalism, the peaceful city with the most violent atmosphere, the city well occupied by terrorists. Silence is just a word in the books here and now we are here to meet our man in action, our Bheema- Bhargava.

It's been almost 14 hours after the president's kidnap and Nandini ma'am has given me the responsibility to bring Bhargava from Kashmir while she is on her way to meet Akanksha in Chennai. I am happy and excited because I am goanna meet my friend Bhargava after almost 10 years. So, when I landed in Kashmir one of the commandos of force-one had come to receive me and he is goanna guide me to Bhargava. Let me tell you about myself first. I am a software engineer basically and was not interested in doing a routine job, I like challenges in the job and that job has to be helpful to people who live around me. That's the reason I chose to be one of the tech-men in I.I.A. so you people might be wondering if I am a hacker, yes I am but not exactly. I handle the database of people. For example, I have face recognition software that scans the image of the person and matches it with their identity, Cool right!? Not only face but also fingerprints, eye lenses, voice recognition, etc. All the information of any suspect is at my fingertips. The name is Tekale, Anupam Tekale. I am an expert in my field, not that experienced but highly talented and that's the reason I was selected for mission 2020 which ruined my career. I hated that year. Worst ever just Nightmares every day. Difficult times though.

I think we reached his home, so, let me introduce you all to my dear friend Bhargava. He has a great house; you have to be lucky enough to own a house in Kashmir. His doors were wide open. It seemed weird. I entered his house and was screaming his name "Bhargava". His house seemed to be completely unorganized, his shoes were in the kitchen sink, the books were on the dining table and the wine bottles were rolling in the living room, T.V. is on and he was lying down on the floor of a bathroom with shower on. With the help of the commando, I brought him to the couch and waited until he woke up. This guy whom I see now was a man of discipline. He use to scream at people for not polishing shoes or not having proper haircuts or not placing things in order. Now, he became a person whom I can never imagine and I blame 2020 for this. He is an aggressive person. His weakness is his anger. In an important operation in 2018, he killed 3 important ISIS terrorists blacklisted by the F.B.I. to save 4 R.A.W. agents and he was honored by a demotion to work as on field officer in I.I.A, that's how he had become a part of I.I.A. and an important pillar in mission 2020.

His eyes slowly started to blink and he was able to see me and said, "Hey Anupam long time man, and thanks, or else I would be in the shower bathing the whole day". I replied, "Never mind old friend, no one home, are you staying alone". He replied, "My wife left me after my suspension and you know it hurts a lot even when your dear is not with you in tough times”. I said, "Yeah, but sometimes we have to face a few tough situations alone". He gave me a suspicious look and said "What brings you here after 10 years?". I said, "You know I heard about your suspension so, I was a bit concerned". He smiled "You think I am a fool it's my 3rd suspension and you came here with concern". He made his face red and took a gun and pointed the gun at my forehead and asked "Tell me or you are gone". My legs started dancing with sweat and with fear said "I.I.A. has a mission for you- The President had been kidnapped and Nandini ma'am wants you to be part of the team". He started laughing and even I was pretending as if I was laughing and he replied, "No, I left the job and I am not and never want to be part of any missions, especially I.I.A". I was shocked after listening that he had quit and replied "What, you had quit the job?". He replied "Yes, and I am going to submit my letter of resignation to Force-one tomorrow". I started clapping and said, "You are not who you were; this is not the Bhargava I knew, that person was completely different". Bhargava in rage "I am the same, the same old person with the same old problems, people told me to change but why should I change when I believe the track I am going is right? 3 days back I killed a terrorist who was the most wanted and you have no idea how many people he killed. how much damage he did to the victim's families and I caught him and if he was arrested you know what the government does, they feed him, thinking that he gives them some information, but no he takes the advantage of the situation, he feels relaxed as if he is in a 5-star hotel. If he falls sick a highly qualified doctor comes for treatment and you know what happens finally... few terrorists hijack a plane or school and demand his release and you know what they do after his release they kill more people. That's the reason I killed him and enjoyed it while I am firing every bullet from my pistol. And after executing him what did the Indian Army call me...they called me 'A MAD MAN' and told me that I have some metal health issues, I have to go to a physiatrist for 10 sittings and you know what, I told them to f*** off. It's not me who has those issues, it's them. They will never understand, that's the reason I am quitting my job".

I continued clapping and said, "you remember when you told me about your demotion from R.A.W. to I.I.A, if I was in that place I would leave the job but you know what you told, you said leaving the job is not the way, you have to prove your worth and most importantly prove them wrong that's what I believe and also said that you love this country and it's security is your responsibility, that's the person I am supposed to meet, not this drunken coward bathing in shower unconcious". I left the house and tried to called Nandini ma'am and wanted to explained the situation but to my surprise I saw a man who is dressed as an official with shoes polished. I had cut the call and he had come near me and told "Hey buddy let's go for the hunt". That was the person I was looking for, Bhargava. Commando beside me was shocked and said, "Sir, there is a bomb planted on the Srinagar-Jammu highway". Bhargava to commando "Is he there in that location?". Commando replied, "Yes he is". Bhargava to commando "Then why fear". I did not understand whom they are reffering to and asked Bhargava "Who is **he** in that location?". Bhargava replied, "Witness that man in action".

Bhargava has the steering and there is an emergency and now this is the most-deadly combo. He started the car and we reached that place in 18 minutes and for ordinary drivers like me, it takes at least 30 minutes. Everyone in that bomb site were biting their nails and the captain is like "everyone alert". I saw a person in a bomber suit with a walkie-talkie in his hand and a cup of unfinished tea near the bomb and was diffusing it. That man started removing the bomb's layer and moving his hands on the wires as if he is tearing papers and on the walkie-talkie, he says "This seems to be a 3 sec time bomb which means this bomb can be diffused only when the clock shows 3 or less than 3 seconds left. So, we have 5 minutes left, record this for a case study and so far we never dealt with a bomb like this but yeah I have read about these kinds. Fine talking about its internal structure, it has many black wires, a red and a green wire as well, now these kinds of bombs don't have specific wire to be cut. So if any one of them is cut wrong, the bomb explodes and if not cut at all, the bomb still explodes". Commando responds "So, what to do". That man replies "this bomb's radius is about 2km so you people stand back, 3 minutes left, fine and now move". Everyone ran as far as they can and I couldn't take my eyes off that man, he was looking so casual even after knowing he is gonna die. The bomb timer hits 2.59 minutes left. That voice on the walkie-talkie seemed like Chakit's and I asked Bhargava "Is it Chakit?". Bhargava said, "Are you sure?". I replied, "Ok let me run a test". I shouted, "Hey man with the bomber suit why are the stadiums so cool?". The man in a bomber suit shouted, "Because there are a lot of fans". He saw me and was like "Hey Anupam how are you". I replied, "Fine what about you, Chakit are you still single". Chakit replied, "I am dating a girl named Rita and she seems to be my type". Commando on walkie-talkie "Can you guys talk about this later after diffusing the bomb". Chakit replied, "Sorry, on duty sir".

Let me tell you about this man Chakit, he is so casual, a big flirt and a bomb expert. His dressing style had a different fanbase, he follows the trend and adapts according to the changing lifestyle, in simple words a cool guy with a brilliant mind. His work is all about diffusing bombs. This man has the knowledge to diffuse almost all 309 types of bombs. He is specific about the bomb's structure, composition, and materials used. Then he comes to the conclusion about what type of bomb it is and then he moves his tools and diffuses it on time and never failed. Even in 2020, he didn't fail. He worked as the captain of the bomb squad in mission 2020 as his first case and he was a beginner and even I was a beginner but not as popular as him. Currently, one of the finest bomb diffusers in the country, and his work is used in case studies for upcoming officers.

The timer is 5.....4......3......2 and everyone praying to God, Chakit on a walkie-talkie says "BOOM we are safe" and he laughs. Chakit to Anupam, "Wassup Lame been so long almost 10 years". I replied, "I had come by walk, so it took nearly ten years". Bhargava said, "Worst joke ever, let me handle this,uff ok, Anupam where next?". I replied "Delhi". Bhargava lifts Chakit on his shoulders and said out of frustration, "Let's explain everything on the way and no need to take his approval, understand". I hope Nandini ma'am convinced Akanksha, meanwhile Chakit started screaming "Anyone help". I was like thank god for this beautiful event. We are on our way to Delhi. We are coming.

CHAPTER III

2020- The Beginning

Narration- Nandini

I am on my way to Chennai. Boarded the flight on time and took my seat. I am kind of stressed, like I don't know if I can do this but I have to, no choice left. A fear started building up whose reasons date back to 2020. Those incidents make your hand shiver the moment you just read or hear about them. Just imagine I was the one who witnessed those incidents and lead that operation. Those deaths, those screams, that blood, no, it's not that easy letting that year pass. It's been 10 years but its impact remains. It's been 14 hours since the President went missing. I guess Anupam has boarded his flight to Kashmir.

That news about the President's kidnap and the Prime minister's press meet reminded me of the night in 2020. It was a normal day like wearing masks, using sanitizers, and social distancing these things were normal during 2020. You know the reason. During those so-called normal days, the Prime minister of that time declared a lockdown in the country. Only necessities like health, food, and bank were available. Media was active and OTT became the new theatres. I was in my home in Delhi self-quarantined and then I got a call from KC, he was so tensed and said there is an emergency, so I had to rush to the NIA head office and reached KC's cabin. KC, "Something big is going to happen in these tough times". Me, "Bigger than Covid-19". KC, "Far more you can imagine". Me, "Details". KC handed a file to me and said, "Intelligence report, huge amount of RDX has crossed our borders and it's said that it can almost blow a city out from the map. RAW has also reported that the probability of terrorist activities might increase and now the RDX and RAW sums up and we are on the edge of losing a city". I looked into the files, "Any reasons or demands they have or motives". KC, "No, we have nothing on them so far. The attack will be a surprise for sure and We have to find that out as soon as possible". Me, "Anything else". KC, "The target city is Hyderabad, reported Bhargava, one of the officers. He will accompany you in Hyderabad and you will be allotted a team and lead this operation and save the city". Me, "What about my daughter?". KC, "I will take care of her I promise. You have a flight tomorrow so be ready, I trust you". Me, "You have no choice, fine then I will leave". KC, "All the best".

10 years back I went on a mission from Delhi to Hyderabad with the responsibility of saving the city but now whenever I travel on a flight it still reminds me of that day, even now. The next day morning I reached Hyderabad and immediately went to the office. I have no idea about the team I was given but I have to handle this. Should do whatever I can to protect these people. I received a fax about the details of the people who are working on the mission. Anupam the techie, Bhargava ex RAW agent, Suhaas IPS and let me introduce you to Akanksha. She had played a major role in the mission. She was a gold medalist in ethical hacking. She tracks in seconds. She types the code effortlessly with a style, she is quick. During her training sessions, she made an algorithm that tracks active bombs which is the first in India. That algorithm was a masterpiece. Probably that algorithm was one of the reasons for her selection in Mission 2020. It was the first time I met them.

I was hiding my anxiety with my anger and was behaving as if I am a strict principal in old films who use only one expression to convey any message and that's annoying. I know but I have to maintain an attitude because I am the Head and with that attitude, I gave my first speech "Guys we are here to deal with the terrorists and we have no clue about what the attack is. It's our responsibility to figure out the problem and also the solution. If we fail then there is no use to run an organization like this. We work to protect and now it's time". Not bad actually, it was fine. Then turned to Akanksha and asked, "Hey, I heard that you own an algorithm that tracks bombs, pretty interesting so how does this work can you explain to the team". She was a little excited and started explaining about it, “Simple this algorithm tracks the bombs, location not exactly but to a particular range and this algorithm tracks the bombs only if they are active”. Impressed actually but still had a question in my mind, “What about inactive bombs then?”. She replied, "No ma‘am, this algorithm works on a mechanism which involves...". I know this is going to take long with those technical terms which I can’t understand, I stopped her and turned towards Bhargava and asked, "Tell me exactly what you got?". Bhargava, "Ma’am according to RAW, the attack will take place in Hyderabad, but what kind we are clueless, and if you see these images, a truck from Srinagar had entered Hyderabad via NH47 and suddenly went missing as soon as it entered Hyderabad, so I assume that this might be the one with the explosives”. I replied, “Any strong lead to prove these assumptions, correct?”. Bhargava, “The men who were in Truck might prove it”. I asked, “You got names”. Bhargava, “not names but I have the photographs”.

I took those photographs and asked Anupam to run a few tests on his weird but amazing laptop. Anupam, "Gotcha, Imran, Soheil, and Kadir”. Me, “Any criminal records?”. Anupam, “Active participants in anti-national activities, also involved in human trafficking of minors to Pakistan and also involved in smuggling of illegal weapons. Active in Baluchistan in Kashmir". Bhargava, "Track his details, run a few background checks". Anupam, "On it, this Imran’s wife is from Hyderabad so he often visits this place". I was overthinking, "So how can we consider him as our suspect without enough evidence". A voice, "first let’s get him and then discuss the evidence”. I was shocked and I was turning back and praying, “Not Dinesh not him” and God was not so kind unfortunately it is Dinesh. Ok, but why?

Fine. I went to a corner and called KC, "Dinesh seriously Dinesh?". Kc, "I hope you like the surprise". I replied, "Dude, if he does something out of the box, I am goanna kick you first for sure. Not convinced with him in the team". KC, "Sometimes you have to push your limits, and for that, you need to go out of the box and do some heroic stuff to catch those villains hiding in the dark". I was convinced and cut the call and went towards the team, they all were chilling and having fun and on the other side, the city is about to burn, "Hello guys get back to work. So, meet Dinesh and be careful". Bhargava, "But why?". Me, "Moving on so Anupam you got their location". Anupam, "Near Charminar". I called Suhaas and told him to raid that place, Suhaas with a low voice, "Impossible, raiding the old city is like you digging your own pit. The unity they have, we can't control them. Arresting a man is equal to humiliating the entire community. Many criminals reside there because they know they are safe". What should I do. I am like everything is gone out of hand with that kind of mood I asked, "What should we do now? And by the way where is Dinesh? Shit, get him to me, get him. I know this guy will mess this up, Anupam track his phone, do it immediately". Anupam, "He is on his way to Charminar". I threw my phone and said to myself, "This guy is going to screw the mission". Picked up another phone and called KC and informed about him. Bhargava was quick and was able to catch Dinesh but it was too late the namaz has started in the Mecca Masjid. Dinesh to Bhargav, "Hey I know I am the only stranger here I am Dinesh I.I.A. Mumbai and Nandini ma'am's favorite agent". Bhargava's reply to him, "She said that you were a headache". Dinesh, "Yeah, I am, but for the bad guys. Fine, but do you have a plan". Bhargava, "You are here without a plan? Idiot". Suhaas, "We might go with a rescue mission, target Imran". Dinesh, "So, I can shoot everyone except Imran good plan lets go". Dinesh rushes and Bhargava chasing him, "Son of a bitch stop, Nandini ma'am was right you are a headache". Dinesh, "Keep calm assholes. It's namaz time and none can move for 10mins from their place so get Imran quietly". Bhargava in a very low voice, "Everyone, keep calm, let's get Imran". They raided his place and found RDX and arrested Imran properly with proof and along with Imran we got Kadir as well. They were brought to the IIA office successfully and everyone was happy that we did it. Suhas, "This was the first ever mission which happened in that area peacefully without any disturbances. Big fan man, Dinesh". Kc called me, "Hey any update Nandini?". I replied, "Sarcasm huh, he should inform me that he is gonna do something, how can he leave me in a dilemma, dude just gave me a heart attack". KC, "He is your favorite, isn't he". I replied, "Yes, he is. Keep it a secret". KC, "Sure enjoy your success".

We all were celebrating, only Dinesh was silent and didn't speak a thing. I asked him, "I have to be in your place and you have to enjoy coz the amount of suspense you had put me in, you deserve a punishment". Dinesh replied, "Maybe but just a thought, this is'nt supposed to end like this. I expected a fight, chase, guns, blood, and bullets it seems peaceful". I said, "Shut up, you are, you have to be on the other side you ended up here accidentally". Dinesh said, "Side of effects of Patriotism". I said, "Chill enjoy". Dinesh, "But seriously I think something is missing like you have to consider this point". Akanksha, "Ma'am there is a red dot in my system". Dinesh asked, "What does it mean?". She replied, "The red dot is a sign which detects a presence of an active bomb". I was shocked and turned to Dinesh, "You were right". Dinesh replied, "...

The flight landed in Chennai. Ok now let's come back to 2030. 16 hours since the president went missing. Akanksha, I am coming.

CHAPTER IV

The Bomb

Narration: Akanksha

The gateway of southern India. The Coastal city with beautiful architectural wonders. The capital city of Tamil Nadu. Once upon a time called Madras and now 'Chennai'. Let me introduce myself I am Akanksha. I am a housewife. So, I lead the least interesting life. My daily activities include cooking, preparing lunch boxes for my husband, pressing my son's shirt, and feeding him, this boy is a real headache in my life. It's been 7 years since my marriage. Learned many things like making Sambhar. My husband left for the office and my son to school and now I am alone watching Vanathai Pola my favorite serial and a new season of big boss has already started so I am good. Suddenly my cooker started to whistle so I had to go to the kitchen and then heard a bell ring, I said, "Kathiru", which means "wait". Then, I opened the door, and oh my god, I closed the door immediately. It was Nandini. No not again. I am not opening the door.

Nandini, "Open the door maa, I am here to talk about something important". I said, "No, I am not interested, you can leave. I am happy here please don't ruin it". Then Nandini asked, "Your eyes don't lie, you still get those visuals yes or no, the time you spend alone, those incidents haunt you, don't they?". I said "Not much". Nandini said, "You know what, I still get them, and every time I get those visuals I always wanted a chance to stop that thing which happened 10 years back, but we can't, all I was waiting for my entire life was for that one chance to prove ourselves, we all are a team of brilliant people who can do wonders, just understand". I said, "I don't want any chances, I am tired please". Nandini, "let me in please". I had no option but to let her in, she entered the house and was like, "The topper of Computer science engineering, fastest fingers, no.1 position, created an algorithm which tracks bombs and now you cook sambhar, you press your husband's clothes". I replied, " cleaning your own mess is far better than trying to clean country's". After hearing this she replied, "well said, I am convinced but at this point of time, we need you". I asked, "You need me or my algorithm, if it's for the algorithm I will give it you happily, take it and never return". She said, "If it's for the algorithm I would either call you or will send another person, because I am sure that if it's for the algorithm you would just give it, why would I come for it, because I want your algorithm along with you. I still remember the day you interrupted our celebrations and told me and Dinesh about that red dot". I still remember that incident. How can I forget that?

10 years back, we were celebrating the arrest of Imran and then I went to switch off my system to save the electricity and suddenly saw a red dot. I was shocked, refreshed, and restarted and yes it still remained red. I rushed towards the team and informed them that I spotted a red dot on my system. Everyone is on it. The location is somewhere in Uppal. We all rushed there, Chakith was ready with his bomb squad and all the measures were taken. Nandini to Chakith, "What's the situation?". Chakith, "We can diffuse the bomb but takes time. The bomb will be activated by a remote whose control will not exceed more than a 2 Km radius. Better get him coz we never know. Prepare for the worst". Nandini to Bhargava, "Go along with Suhaas and Dinesh, if you find anyone suspicious, check them". Dinesh, "We might need the residence record?". Nandini, "Do it fast. We don't have much time". Dinesh went on checking the residence list, Bhargava and Suhaas were looking for someone suspicious, and then suddenly Dinesh got a call, he had cut that call. He got it again. He declined it again. His phone rang once again and irritated Dinesh lifted the call and some voice, "Jeena Yahan Marna Yahan iske siva Jana kahan". He had cut the call and there was a blink of a red dot somewhere in the System, I informed Nandini immediately she was like, "Chill you are tensed we are all here don't worry". Then I told her, "Ma'am the dot was present for 2 seconds, something might have happened in that place". Nandini, "Might be a glitch". I was continuously after her, "It says Begumpet". Nandini

in anger, "Shut up Akanksha". She got a call from KC and at the same time Suhaas rushed towards her, Nandini stopped him and lifted the call. Suhaas and KC at the same time, "There was a bomb blast in Begumpet". Nandini dropped her phone after listening to this. Dinesh rushed towards Nandini and said that he found the man but everyone was in shock and Dinesh asked, "What happened?". Akanksha, "There was a blast in Begumpet housing society". After a few seconds, "There is another red dot". Dinesh, "Where?". I replied, "The opposite building and the red dot in this building have vanished". Chakith, "The bomb is inactive right now and we can't diffuse inactive bombs ". Nandini, "Chakith, there is a bomb in the opposite building, go get it". Everyone rushed to the opposite building, Anupam tracked the list of suspicious people, Suhaas checked everyone but none had a remote and their phones were taken. The bomb in the opposite building was diffused and then Dinesh got a call again, he had cut the call, it repeated twice, and then he lifted the call and again with the same voice, "Jeena Yahan marna Yahan iske siva jana kahan. Heyy don't cut the call, turn back.... what do you see". Dinesh replied, "A building". The red dot appeared in my system which detected the active bomb in the building again. The voice on the call, "I guess you are having a blast old friend, bye". The bomb had exploded. It was unexpected and Chakith came out with good news of diffusing the bomb but after looking at the picture opposite to him, he remained silent. Dinesh called that number but it switched off, he tried again and again and again but no use he just threw his phone and screamed out so loud meanwhile, KC called Nandini and asked, "What's happening in Hyderabad?". Nandini replied, "KC please give me some time, I will talk to you about this". Bhargava, "Guys check if there are any more explosives or bombs in this area. We need to clear this out as soon as possible". Nandini ma'am was literally in tears.

Let's get back to 2030, I asked her, "Yeah I remember that day in detail". She asked, "You saw it, you still see it. You always wanted to rewrite that day in your life, don't you? But we can't. Now we got a chance to prove ourselves that we are not losers. We now have a chance to prove what we are. If you miss this, you will regret this all your life". I was convinced. I am not a loser. I always wanted a chance, and now I have it, why should I let it go, then my husband texted me, "hey honey, did you have your lunch. I am busy can you pick up our kid from school". Now again I realize I have a family. So, what should I do now. I told her that I need time and in response to it she said, "Here take your ticket to Delhi and your letter of joining to IIA, I will be waiting for you in the airport. Fine I'll leave then". She left and I am in a dilemma should I leave or not. I called my Husband and asked him, "I wanted to tell you something". My husband was like I am busy talk to you later. I said, "It's urgent". My husband said, "you have 5 minutes". I told him that I am considering to join my old job. My Husband in frustration replied, "Are you out of your mind? Listen go pick up the kid on time. Cook and feed him. That's your job understand. I am earning right". I replied, "This is not about earning, it's about proving my worth". He replied, "You cook well, really tasty. I know your worth. So, concentrate on making sambhar, not on computer codes and algorithms". I requested him, "Please I never asked you anything since our wedding. Please". He was not in a good mood and at once I said, "Listen now listen to me. Press your clothes. Cook your sambhar and don't forget to feed our Kid because I have decided to go back to my old job because that's where I belong and that's what I deserve". He replied, "Fine, go kill more people". I said, "Yeah, I will go for sure not kill but to protect and one last thing. Pick our boy from school because I am busy. I cut the call. Took my old laptop, packed my bag, signed the letter and now I am joining the IIA. I am going to the airport.

Reached the airport and spotted Nandini and hugged her and said, "I am back". She responded, "Yes I can see that". I asked her, "What next?". And she replied, "The boys are on their way to Delhi just boarded the flight now it's our turn. 20 hours since the president went missing". We are coming don't worry Mr. President and we boarded our flight.

CHAPTER V

The Game begins

Narration: Chakith

Bhargava forcefully took me to the airport and we boarded the flight to Delhi and explained me the whole scenario. Ok, so Bhargava, the President was missing for the past 20hrs and Nandini ma'am voluntarily went and spoke to the head of IIA to start an unofficial mission that includes our team that's me, you, Anupam, and Akanksha, right? So, we are on our way to Delhi. I am waiting for this, it is the time to prove my worth. Losers, they all called us losers. I diffused that bomb that day but the bomb opposite to me was a surprise. I still remember the scene, the screams of Dinesh, and silence of Nandini, she stood like a statue of disappointment.

10 years back, the sound of the blast was not new and its effect is something I had experienced before, but this one this is not ordinary. Nandini got a call from KC but she refused to speak on the spot. Bhargava ordered Suhaas and his men to check the entire region for any explosives and after a clear check and damage control we left from the spot. After reaching the office KC called Nandini and she explained everything that happened. Suhaas faced the media and its, questions. Suhaas started his interaction with the press by saying, "Citizens I can understand your concern but our country is in a tough time, first the COVID-19 and now the attacks, this year sucks but we all have to be prepared because we can't everytime monitor or find out the exact location of the bombs and get them, it's you who have to keep a look on your surroundings and report any suspicious activity to '7386704325', and I am not here to answer any of your questions so just stay home and stay safe". Reporter in news "How can people expect to stay at home to be safe". He replied, "See, we are doing what we

can, but every suspicious activity can't be tracked it's practically impossible man, it's your responsibility, your life is in your hands if you find something suspicious, call to this damn number on the screen, please present this number on your channels instead of following a celebrity or some stupid story which makes no sense. Thank you".

Bhargava was a little irritated, definitely not little, but sufficient to blame the tech team for not doing their job properly and the argument started between him and Akanksha, Bhargava called that algorithm of Akanksha a piece of shit and in return, she said, "You guys at least diffused one bomb because of that algorithm or else you guys had no clue where the bomb would be". Fair point actually, but Bhargava is in no mood to consider any logics, all he wants is to win the argument and Nandini meanwhile spoke to KC and was irritated and after seeing these guys fight, she threw a vase to stop them and said, "Enough, accept we failed. Out of 3 we could diffuse one at least and the happiest part is no one's in that building but what happened in Begumpet was". Dinesh interrupts and asks me, "The control of the bomb was within a 2km radius right". I replied, "Yes" and then he asked Anupam, "We went through the details of all the residents right". Anupam replied, "Yes we did". Dinesh asked Bhargava, "You were the one who took the resident's list". Bhargava replied, "Yeah I took it from the security guard". He went closer to Bhargava and asked, "Come again". Bhargava, "I took it from the security guard". Dinesh holds Bhargava's collar and said, "That asshole had the remote, it was him who had the control". Nandini to Dinesh, "Don't talk rubbish". Dinesh in response, "Uff rubbish, fine Anupam get the details of the security guard". Anupam, "Nothing on him". Dinesh, "Something cc camera footage". Anupam, "He was wearing a mask, fuck corona fuck Chinese, fine let me check his lens, forehead pattern or Bhargava do you have that book so that we can get his fingerprints". Bhargava, "Yeah here you go". Anupam ran a few tests and finally came to a conclusion and said, "Dinesh was right, we got Imran and Kadir but this one is Soheil".

Dinesh, “I knew it”. Nandini, “So, Soheil was the man behind the scene”. Dinesh, “No no no no. Soheil was just a piece on the board. There was someone. Someone behind this. That someone called me and sang a song. He was a good singer but a sinner”. Nandini, "Who?". Dinesh, "I don’t know, the way he had run this thing, I rate him 10/10. He confused us like hell. At first, he diverted us to Imran he made us think that it was over but immediately after that, he planted a bomb which was almost 7km away from our office, then a red dot in Begumpet which is like 14kms away from the place he initially planted the bomb. Let’s assume that our office is at A and the distance from the office to Uppal is ’x‘ and similarly, the distance between our office to Begumpet is also ’x‘ and now from Uppal to Begumpet, the distance is twice ’x‘ i.e ’2x‘ so even if tried we couldn’t. He won. He played with the algorithm like a small kid playing with a smartphone. Genius". Nandini, "So, what do you want to say?". Dinesh, "He is not gonna stop with this one attack. I heard his voice. Didn’t speak but as quite sufficient to judge what kind of a guy he is. That confidence and , he indirectly gave us a hint that this is just the beginning. So, we have to be prepared for the next attack. We have to split and work or else we will end up like this again. Prepare for the worst”. Nandini, “Why did he call you?”. Dinesh replied, “To warn me to be careful because he is goanna attack and had wished me all the best”. Nandini, “Who does that?”. Dinesh replied, “He, my old friend. That’s what he said at the end. Old friend”. Anupam, “Dinesh you are getting an anonymous call”. Dinesh, “Lift the call and let me handle it”. The call was attended.

Unknown voice: jeena yahan marna yahan iske sivva janna kahan....

Dinesh: I know it’s you

Unknown voice: Who am I

Dinesh: An unknown person hiding in dark.

Unknown voice: hey hey I never hide in the dark, I just occupy the light and fill it with dark.

Dinesh: Ok you are confusing.

The unknown voice: I am not. I am straightforward, this society finds me confusing because it can never accept me because of its weird ideologies.

Dinesh: Ok, so I am not gonna ask why but what are your demands? Like, do you guys have some motive behind these activities?

Unknown voice: Few childhood memories. Yes, they haunt.

Dinesh: Whatever you are doing is not right. So, stop.

Unknown voice: Is this a sort of warning? So, what I am going to get if I don't?

Dinesh: Death.

Unknown voice: Death (laughs) So, death it is huh? Let me tell you something. The day we meet, you want to kill me, You want me dead so badly but you cannot because your hands will be tied so hard that even if you have a chance to kill me you refuse to do it.

Dinesh: Daydreaming huh?

Unknown voice: It's almost 7. Wait, intelligent guy. You got my location right

Dinesh: You are either an absolute idiot or a retarded genius. You know how many lives were lost, how many people were injured, and the damage you caused.

Unknown voice: calm down pal I just did it to introduce myself to the city and by myself means "The fear". I just introduced fear to a peaceful society I had just given an introduction, **the game is going to begin and starts with the rise of sun which mutes the voice of society**, and you guys have nothing to hear except the cries of the brave and mourns of the dead.

(cuts the call)

Dinesh, "Hello hello". Nandini, "Who the hell is this psychopath?". Dinesh to Anupam, "Did you record the entire conversation?". Anupam responded, "Yes, I did". Dinesh, "Let's decode it. He might leave some clues like the location. He is in Hyderabad. So Anupam gets the list of all the newcomers to the city, and Suhaas enquires everyone. We almost got the big fish. Nandini, call KC. Nandini calls KC, "Dinesh wants to speak". KC to Dinesh, "What?". Dinesh, "Sir, the main guy behind the master plan is in the city. Stop every car every bus every train every flight now. We need to get him". KC, "I will have a word with the PM and the C.M. now. On it Dinesh". Dinesh to Akanksha, "Play the conversation". Nandini was busy convincing the C.M. meanwhile Dinesh, Akanksha, and I were listening to the Audio and Bhargava was assisting Suhaas. We got something. He said that the game is going to begin and starts when light first appears from the sky which mutes the voice of society. So, what is the voice of society? I guess Bhargava had an answer...

The flight had landed. 22 hours since the President went missing. Back to 2030. So Nandini ma'am is on her way. Me to Anupam, "It's almost been 10 years right". Anupam, "Yeah 10 years nostalgia. Memories". Bhargava, "They are no memories idiots they are nightmares". Ok, calm down angry bird. The man had a point they are no memories they were nightmares.

CHAPTER VI

The Riddle

Narration: Bhargava

Waiting for Nandini to come. 22 hours since the President went missing. I went to KFC to eat something and I saw the person at the counter solving puzzles with the help of few hints given. Solving puzzles is not something new. There was a day when we decoded a riddle where some hundreds of lives depended on the answer to that puzzle.

I still remember the room which was filled with tension. His words were something like **the game is going to begin and starts with the rise of sun which mutes the voice of society**. I started to think. So, he meant morning. The game means the attack so the attack starts in the morning. Next, which mutes the voice of society. Ok morning, voice, society. What sound do we hear in the morning? Namaz. It's Sunday tomorrow. Church bell. What about temples, suprabath, etc happens in the early morning right? Ok, but with this pandemic who is visiting temples? I explained this to Dinesh, Akanksha and Chakith. Dinesh, "What's the point of planning an attack where there are no public gatherings?". Chakith," Dinesh the last attack was not in a public place, it was an apartment, a residential area". Dinesh, "Akanksha, I need a list of all the holy places in Hyderabad now". Akanksha, "On it, yeah we have 1067 from small to big". Bhargava, "It's a huge number, Shortlist them by the number of residential areas within their range with a huge population". Akanksha, "Around 200". Bhargava," shortlist them by the size 'big' come on". Akanksha, "40". Bhargava, "look for the active bombs in those 40 locations". Akanksha, "Zero". Dinesh, "So what's the plan?". Bhargava, "We need a constant watch on those 40 areas. Check everywhere we have time until the morning 12'o clock. Sunrises at 6:45 max so we have 6 hours 45 minutes left. Start the mission. Divide and conquer". Dinesh, "Roger that". Nandini,

"We got the permission for 72 hours, the CM is declaring a lockdown exclusively for our work, so all you guys got is 72 hours". Dinesh called the team and explained the plan. The entire police team had divided and started their search in those 40 areas along with Dinesh, Bhargava, Nandini, and Chakith. The clock was ticking but we didn't find a thing. It's almost 5:40 in the morning, we got nothing in our hands. Akanksha was refreshing her system since 12 but got nothing. Anupam was watching *Jab we met* on some channel and Akanksha snatched his remote and changed the channel, there appeared some news channel where the reporter said, "Yesterday what Suhaas said was controversial. We care for the public we are for the public and We are the voice of the society". Akanksha to Anupam, "He just said the voice of society. He meant the media, the media had many employees working for them in numbers". Anupam had sent us a message 'code red'. It means there is an emergence of a high level.

We were screwed. I called Dinesh immediately, he was in Birla Mandir. I called him and said, "Dinesh we were wrong". Dinesh said "What?". I said, "Listen, the voice of the society means media or press, I just saw it on T.V. I am damn sure about it look at this video". I had sent this video and Dinesh said "The time is 6:15 do something, ok first let's connect all the team members, fast, do it". I connected everyone and we were on a conference "Ok guys listen we screwed up, change in plans the hotspots are not the holy places they are Press and news channels and now we have 15 minutes, and the sun might rise early".

Anupam said, "They are 30 news channel studios so yeah just divide the teams . I will just send you people the location of the nearest news channel and just rush". We can see the sun coming out, the light started flowing in the sky. One misunderstanding was about to lead to big destruction and then a news channel texted all the studios to vacate as an emergency but meanwhile, the guards of the studio who were actually terrorists started firing on the location, this was shared with all the teams and were rushing, luckily it was nearer to Bhargava's site and Dinesh suspected something else he immediately ordered the bomb squad leading Chakit to check the opposite and nearer buildings and he got bombs which were inactive Chakit dismantled the bombs and found the persons operating them and they are taken in the custody the terrorists were encountered with the help of army support from AOC, thanks to Nandini and KC. 15 deaths, and 60 injuries. The damage was not much, but was done. The other media channels started broadcasting this in their news even though we warned them to leave.

Anupam was trying to track the call of last night he made 3 attempts with 3 different methods but resulted in nothing and Akanksha was just updating the algorithm for tracking the bomb's exact GPS location and got an alert with a red spot, on other news channel's office which 7km far away from the location. She called Dinesh immediately and told "Dinesh code red emergency bomb planted in the News X office location 7 km far and I don't know what time does the bomb explodes". Dinesh "Son of a bitch Suhaas, inform News X that there is a bomb at the NEWS X office call them tell them and tell them to vacate now, Bhargava move the car". Suhaas informed the News X office and the surroundings and then the bomb exploded. Dinesh called me "Bhargava where are you?". He was on his way. I met Dinesh and we both started rushing toward News X.

Suddenly she saw another red spot in the algorithm and said "Mission abort, I repeat abort, divert it to TV-news the bomb had already exploded at News X". Dinesh said, "Bhargava divert to TV-news office take a U-turn fast Anupam Guide us, idiot". Anupam said, "Cool guys I had sent the shortest route you better take a bike". Dinesh said, "Are you out of your mind ok, Bhargava stop that man in the blue shirt take his keys get that bike what the fuck is he doing when the CM declared a lockdown". Bhargava was driving the bike and Dinesh was on phone sitting behind him. Dinesh said, "Call Chakit and connect to him fast". Anupam said, "Fine fine Connected him". Dinesh, "Chakit ok fine we are near to the location, and guide me to diffuse the bomb". Chakit, "The moment you see the bomb just watch out for timers, if yes then cut the blue wire if no timer, then red and green". Dinesh said, "Fine". Akanksha interrupted "Bomb at NewsTV office". Dinesh said, "What the fuck should I do? Chakit moves to NewsTV now and tell all the members to split and reach all the news channels". Akanksha started getting red spot alerts on all news channel offices and started blinking and she shouted "All news channels tell them to vacate". Suhaas said, "Shit ok I will tell all the press to do it, guys they are bombs in all your offices, call your offices and tell them to vacate fast". Dinesh reached the TV-news office everyone vacated the office. Dinesh diffused the bomb in the TV-news but it was too late for other news channels, every news channel office exploded and there was no time given for the people to vacate. All the bombs and at once boom. It was a massacre. The only channel left was TV-news. Everyone in all the news channel offices vacated so lives were saved but News X. Now there is no news channel except this TV-news unfortunately. That guy literally muted the voice of society. What a day it was. We reached the office. Nandini was tired and said, "Guys what the hell just happened, the guy just attack 30/30 news channels". Dinesh replied, "There was not much loss of life". Nandini, "Don't speak like him. 15 Deaths means 15 families and you know the value of lives more than me". Dinesh, "Don't get me started". Nandini, "You lost your parents in the same attack and you say not much death, what do you mean". Dinesh, "Stop it". Suhaas, "45 deaths including News X". I had to respond so I did, "Out of 300 lives we saved 255 lives, and we also warned the news channels to vacate but they instead started broadcasting it in news and they died due to their foolishness. We are not responsible for that. So guys calm down 255 lives saved". The room is now silent but then suddenly Anupam to Dinesh, "Dinesh you are getting the call from an anonymous number". Dinesh, "Connect me to that asshole immediately give me those damn headphones". Nandini, "Carefull". Call connected.

Unknown voice: la la la la lalala lalala...

Dinesh: Ok fine now what?

Unknown voice: How's the gift?

Dinesh: You call it a gift. People died, many injured. Think about the families you affected, and you laugh. You laugh at death.

The unknown voice: The only difference between a madman and a normal person is how he treats the dead. Normal person mourn but a madman like me enjoy. You know what's more satisfying than those death the fear in the eyes of people who are alive and saw those deaths, those helpless tears and the worst part is they don't even know who is next, might be him, his relatives or neighbor. See how chaotic it is, such a beautiful panic environment created. I just hate a calm city, I love to watch a panicked atmosphere filled with fear and tension.

Dinesh: What do you want? What do you demand? We are ready to provide you with whatever you need. Tell me your demands

Unknown voice: I am already getting what I want. So, there's nothing you can give me.

Dinesh: Who the hell are you?

Unknown voice: I already told you.. an old friend

Dinesh: What. I am in no mood for your jokes and tired of your stupid riddles.

Unknown voice: St. Pauls?

Dinesh: That's my school..

Unknown voice: Ye dosthi hum nahi thodenge...

Dinesh: Aditya!?

(call cuts)

Nandini, "You know him". Dinesh, "Long story, story of an old friend".

23 hours since the president went missing...

• • •

CHAPTER VII

An Old Friend

Narration: Dinesh

Mountains, greenery, fresh air, and the most peaceful place in the entire country. After many traumatic incidents, I made this place my home. One of the northeastern states is 'Mizoram'. 28th October 2030. It's early in the morning but I have to wake up as I have a few very important household chores to do. Went to my desk checked my gun and its bullets, loaded the gun and unloaded it again. Walked into the kitchen. Heard a knock, took a knife and reached the main door, and opened it. It was the milkman outside, he delivered the milk and I went back to the kitchen, and started slicing the raw bread with a knife and boiled the milk. Time is almost 7:30. It's school time and my daughter needs to wake up. Her name is Tara. 6 years old. Lost her mom in an accident. An unfortunate incident it was. Fine, it's school time. Went to her bedroom and woke her up, "It's school time, go brush your teeth". Took her to the washroom and made her brush. I went to the kitchen to prepare her lunchbox, and after some time, she came to the dining room and had her breakfast, and I must drop her at school. While dropping her to school I asked her, "Did you make any friends my little princess". She replied, "Yeah many daddy". I said, "Great, school friends are always special". She asked, "Do have any special friends?". I replied, "Yes I did". She asked, "Who?". I replied, "A terrorist". She started laughing, "Dad, you are joking right". I replied, "Yeah, here comes the school, have fun". She gets down from the car and says, "Sure your majesty". Drama queen, cute.

Yes, my friend was a terrorist. 10 years back. I still remember the way I killed that bastard with my gun. His phones calls and his special song "Jeena Yahan marna Yahan" still haunt me. We were good friends. Really good friends. But never expected him to become the person whom he became. Aditya my childhood friend. Back then in 2005 I still have our group photo.

2005, St Paul's High School 5th standard, I was an orphan, my parents died in a terrorist attack in Kashmir. I was saved by the army and from that day onwards I decided to save the people from the demons wearing the mask of humans. An army officer named Nilesh Agarwal was made my legal guardian. I thank him for all he did to me. So, during my school days, a some random guy entered my class, he was new admission. He was so nervous while introducing himself. So, everyone in the class started making fun of him in the initial stage itself. Even I laughed, I admit it. But as the days passed the bullying was on another level. They used to tear his pocket, steal his lunch, if asked smash his face, and in reverse, they use to complain about him and teachers use to take strict actions. Catholic schools so yeah, the punishments were tough. Standing outside the class in sun, kneeling, etc. Pity that boy. A year passed, completed my 5th with flying colors but he failed, his Parents were called and his father had hit him so hard in front of everyone. I saw him hitting. I said this to Nilesh uncle on a call and I still remember what he said. After explaining everything, he asked me, "What is your goal?". I replied, "To protect the good ones from the bad, to achieve my goal I have to become an army officer". After listening to this he said, "Who are the bad guys?". I replied, "The terrorists". He with a smile said, "Yeah you are right, the terrorists are the bad guys, agreed. Terrorists are the bad guys for the country, so when you become an army officer it's your responsibility to protect the good guys from those so-called bad guys. But for now who are the bad guys?". I replied, "The bullies in our school". He with a smile said, "So, it's your responsibility to protect that good boy from those bad guys, the so-called bullies". I completely understood and replied, "Roger that, Dinesh reporting from Hyderabad sir". He laughed and said, "Ok ok young man, save him from the bad guys".

His words were inspiring, so when the bad guys were bullying Aditya, I went and stopped them, ok details I fought with them. Teachers punished me along with the bad guys and Aditya in the class is listening to her lecture. Even though it was a punishment, it was satisfying. Maybe that's the reason freedom fighters enjoy their sacrifices or going to jail. I liked that feeling. Aditya had come to me and given me a 'Kacha mango bite' and said, "Thank you". I felt like a hero and told him, "Bro, it's my responsibility. Friends". He gave me a handshake. We became friends. In old movies when a friend was in trouble, he calls out the hero's name, same situation here, I was the hero. We use to sing the song from Sholay, "Yeh dosti hum nahi todenge". I use to handle the bullies but marks, teachers use to hit him with a wooden scale. His father use to hit him hard in front of everyone. During my absence, the bullies use to trouble him. One day I asked him about his family, and in tears, he said, "My dad passed away when I was 7 years old. The guy who is beating me is my stepdad. My mom remarried for my future. But he is making it worse. I also have a stepbrother. The situation at home is horrible. What I face in my home is nothing compared to what you see in school". I could do nothing other than feel sad for him. Then after the year 2007, we had a terrorist attack in the school. 7 terrorists with guns attacked the building. Everyone was hiding somewhere safe, Aditya was missing. I was searching for him and suddenly a terrorist spotted me and made me kneel. He pointed the gun toward me. Then I remembered what Nilesh sir use to teach me during my holidays in Kashmir. I attacked his legs, hit his chin with my elbow and snatched his gun, and killed him. That was my first blood. Then with that gun, I protected a few of my schoolmates and then the situation was sorted by the police. And I was awarded the Pradhan Mantri Rashtriya Bal Puraskar for my bravery. Nilesh sir was super proud. I explained this to my team. Nandini after listening to this story she felt sad and said, "He must have a family right. His mother maybe. If we get his mother we might get him".

Anupam tracked the information from St Pauls and we visited Aditya's home but now the house was locked. People in the surroundings said that a family was murdered in this house, and from then, none were interested in buying this house. Fine, something happened, a mystery that none of them knew and only one man can answer my question i.e. Aditya. We arranged an interview with TV-news studio and Suhaas revealed everything I knew about Aditya. After the interview, we received a call from an anonymous number which was obviously from Aditya.

(Call connected)

Me: Hello

Aditya: Yaadon ki baarat nikli hai aaj dil ke dware, Dil ke dware

Me: Sapnon ki shehnai beete dinon ko pukare. Dil ke dware

Aditya: Good old days huh

Me: 13 years, a long time, what happened to that innocent young man? The person you were and the demon you are now, what made you?

Aditya: The person you saw 13 years back was dead in St Paul's. This guy was born from his death.

Me: The person I knew was not like this. I can help you, you were my friend. Surrender. I will help.

Aditya: Help. What help? Oh, the days back when you fought those bullies, oh that was very helpful. Fine, what about the teacher, what about my stepdad and stepbrother? You had no idea what I went through. You know what my stepdad used to hit me with his belt for no reason and whenever my mom comes for my rescue you know what my stepbrother used to do. That asshole was far worse than my stepdad, trust me. Those marksstill remain on my back. Whenever I look at those marks, I feel the pain, and then one fine day my stepdad was watching some film, I still remember that scene. There was a thief who was chased by about 40 people and then he took his pistol and shot a bullet, those 40 people pissed their pants and ran away. I started thinking that one pistol had the power to create a sense of fear in those people then what if I had a gun in my hand? I was waiting for that one day and the day had come. 2007 terrorist attack in St Paul's. Everyone was scared but for me, it was a chance. I went to the head and showed him the cabins where our teachers were hiding, our bullies were hiding and in return, I got a gun and I shot our teacher who hit me with that bloody wooden scale. Before shooting I counted the number of times, he had hit me with a wooden scale, and then I did the same thing to him. I took his wooden scale and had beaten him to death which was satisfying instead of using a gun. Next the bullies I enjoyed killing them with the gun. Started firing them from the legs to the head covering every part front and back. Then the police had come to rescue and along with the leader I escaped. So the leader asked me to join the terrorist group for which I agreed but on one condition. He gave me a fully loaded gun. I went to my home shot my dad on his legs and had removed his belt from his pant, tore his clothes killed him nude by beating him with that belt. My stepbrother woke up and my mom was shocked. He took a knife and kept it near my mom's throat and warned me that if I won't leave, he is going to kill my mom. I was emotional I killed my mom. Collateral damage. Then I caught him pushed the gun barrel in his ass and finished all the bullets in my gun. I went to my mom and said, "Mom if I become a popular terrorist then someone might kidnap you to find me. So, please die for my future. I love you, you did a lot to protect me, enough you deserve better". Killed her. Then I joined the terrorist organization. And had become their commander now.

Me: I understand your childhood was dark

Aditya: Objection,my childhood wasn't dark, the people in my childhood made it. You know what if my stepdad was caring and stepbrother was supportive and classmates were good to me, my days used to be good and I might become a good person. Unfortunately, it's not like any of the above-mentioned qualities. They made me stay in dark, they kept me in dark, and they forced me to be in the dark until I became the dark. It was so dark, that it can swallow the light no matter how bright it is or how powerful it is.

Me: Even now you have a chance, this is not the way

Aditya: Why should I change? Why it's always me? I am not here to change. I will not change. I will get what I want and I am getting it. Dinesh, you were my friend, so stay away from me.

Me: My responsibility is to protect. I will do it even if it includes my death.

Aditya: Then we aren't friends anymore. Enemies. We made a choice. You stay in the light and I stay in dark. One day I promise I will swallow you.

Me: All the best

(Call disconnects)

Let's come back to 2030. Fine just wanted to relax, so I switched on the TV, and the news flashed that the president is missing. It's been 11 hours since the president went missing. 2020 was the latest massacre and then after 10 years, we have the president's kidnap. I was waiting for one chance to prove that team 2020 deserves something much better than what we got right now. I waited and waited and finally yes this is the moment. I immediately called Nandini, "Hey Dinesh here". Nandini, "Why did you call me?". I replied, "Just saw the news President of India went missing". Nandini, "Yeah". I asked, "Are you on the team?". Nandini, "Nope". I told her, "Just a thought about having a 2020 reunion". Nandini, "Are you out of your mind?". I requested her, "Nandini, KC is head of IIA, he is your best friend, he actually had a crush on you during your training days. So, please do something about this". She was not convinced. I gave long motivational speeches but none worked and at last said, "Fine, but ask yourself do we really deserve what we have now. You and I both know that we were the people who had put an end to it. In records, you all labeled it as a failed mission in 2020 but deep inside you know that we saved the city from upcoming threats. The city now we see is because of us. We were labeled as failures, it's our responsibility to prove that we are not what they think". Nandini cuts the call. When Nandini cuts the call, it means she is convinced. After 2 hours I got a call from Nandini that she convinced KC for the team but as a plan B. We are an unofficial team to find the president. Then I booked my ticket to Delhi and reached the airport and checked the crime scene and went to the IIA and met KC and went through some files and reports given so far. And I drove the car to the airport to pick up my team in 2020. I am still waiting for them at the exit.

23 hours since the president went missing...

CHAPTER VIII

The Reunion

Location: Indira Gandhi International Airport. It's been 23 hours since the President went missing.

Team 2020 is going to have it's reunion. Nandini and Akanksha had already landed in Delhi and are waiting at exit no.2. Bhargava is having his food in KFC, and Anupam and Chakith are stalking girls. Wait. Anupam is married, right? *Men will be men.* Meanwhile, Nandini called Anupam and asked, "Hey, where are you guys?". Anupam replied, "Near KFC". Nandini said, "I will meet you guys at exit no. 2, be there". Anupam responded, "Ok". Nandini loudly, "Now". Anupam to Chakith, "Bro Nandini ma'am wants us at exit no. 2, call Bhargava". Chakith with a little fear replies in low tone, "do you really want me to go and disturb Bhargava while he's eating?". Anupam understands the situation and replies, "Fair point wait let me try". Anupam entered KFC sat beside Bhargava and says, "Nandini ma'am wants to meet us at exit 2". Bhargava with a chicken wing in his mouth replies, "Fine then let's go, why waste time? Come on Chakith what are you waiting for..." swallows the meat and started moving his legs faster and also forced Anupam and Chakith to walk at his pace and reached exit no. 2.

Finally, we got Nandini, Akanksha, Chakith, Anupam, and Bhargava together. Everyone was so happy and had a proper conversation after 10 years and then Nandini, "Guys you still have a surprise left". Everyone, "What?". Nandini, "Follow me, something's missing right". Anupam, "Dinesh?". Bhargava, "Where is Dinesh?". Akanksha, "Is he not part of the mission?". And then Dinesh came out of the car, "Namaskar dostho". Chakith, "Namaste anna". Finally, they all gathered. Dinesh, "Fine let's talk but first get in to the car, we have a lot to discuss". Everyone in the car were having a conversation about their life, before and after 2020. Nandini, "Not much, to be honest. Had a couple of successful missions and taking care of my daughter, that's it". Anupam, "Was working in a software company, had a comfortable life, good salary, married my cousin and now I have 2 kids". Bhargava, "Aww how romantic Anupam". Akanksha, "Yeah same but I stopped working for a year and then got married, what about you Bhargava?". Bhargava, "My wife left me because I drink too much". Akanksha, "That's not fair, drinking is no big deal. I am on your side". Bhargava, "What will you do when your husband drinks too much and vomits on the bed daily". Akanksha, "Would definitely divorce him, yuck". Bhargava, "That's what she did". Akanksha, "I take her side now". Chakith, "So everyone here is married, divorced, or had kids except Dinesh and me". Dinesh, "I have a daughter". Chakith, "Great so even Dinesh has a daughter". Dinesh, "I am not her father, she is not my daughter and I am not married". Nandini, "What has happened?". Dinesh stopped the car and gets down and lights a cigarette, Chakith gets down and says, "Hey let me handle the steering chill man, relax breathe in breath out". Chakith sat in the driver's seat and started the car and Dinesh started narrating his story, "After I killed Aditya back in 2020 and when our mission was declared as a failure, I couldn't take it and I decided to leave IIA but the higher authorities had different plans and had posted me in RAW, patriotismtied my hands and back in 2025, I was involved in a mission of capturing Altaf Hussain leader of a radical group who was involved in local attacks in Northeast, so we had information that he was coming to a local restaurant and we were ready to execute our plan and started firing, then, unfortunately, I accidentally shot a woman, she had a 2-year old kid with her. The mission was a success we captured Altaf Hussain. We all succeeded in executing Altaf Hussain but we all failed to stop the tears of that small girl who lost her mother because of one mistake I had committed. We tried to contact her family but there were none from the family who had shown up including her father, So I took responsibility for that girl from that day onwards. I drop her to school, cook her lunch, take her shopping, and help her with homework but the bitter truth is she thinks the man who murdered her mom, is her dad. Whenever she calls me dad, I always have that guilt. If I had a chance to correct my mistakes, it's not 2020, but it's 2025".

Chakith, "we are very sorry". Everyone was feeling sad for Dinesh and Dinesh was like, "Guys chill, we have a mission, it's almost 24 hours since the President went missing". Everyone reaches an unofficial IIA workplace and enters the place. Nandini shares the files regarding the President's missing case and started explaining the incident, "So guys, The President left Russia on 27th October 2030 at 7 PM IST. He landed in Delhi at 2 AM IST and then his car started at 2:30 AM it reached the Rashtrapati Bhavan at 3:13 AM but he didn't make it. All the CC cameras were checked everything was clear except the Sardar Patel Marg. The officers who were escorting him informed him that the path was dark and with smog due to Diwali celebrations. So, we assume that his car went missing somewhere on Sardar Patel Marg. We got no clue, the person behind this planned it very well, he gave us nothing, it's a clean crime without any black spot". Bhargava, "So, the president's car made it to the house but not the President". Nandini, "Yeah, so the assumption here is President went missing in Sardar Patel Marg". Dinesh, "Who was driving the car?". Nandini, "The driver is in the custody but had no clue, they already questioned him". Bhargava, "So how come the president went missing not the Driver?". Anupam, "The president might have jumped from the car lol". Akanksha holds her laugh and Chakith, "This is no time for jokes, control or say it in a low tone so that only I can hear". Anupam, "I am sorry". Dinesh, "Could be, the president has a family so, there might be some threat or anything to them which made him do that". Nandini, "there can be such a possibility". Bhargava, "Assumption no. 2, I doubt the driver, like he had to keep an eye on the president when he is jumping off the car right. If he was off the car, where was he picked then?". Nandini, "Unfortunately there was not much traffic and smog made it worse". Bhargava, "Fine let's assume he jumped off then who closed the door". Chakith, 'the person in the car". Bhargava, "Who was in the car?". Dinesh, "The driver". Bhargava, "Assumption 1 or 2 or n whatever the driver had a role to play in this game. Big role indeed". Nandini, "But IIA got nothing on him". Bhargava, "Let me try". Nandini, "Let's go to the head office".

KC was busy on the phone with the pm, "Sir I know it's been 24 hours we are getting close, and give us another 24 hours we might get President". PM, "Look this is no game, it's the President who went missing get him as soon as possible". KC, "sure sir". Nandini knocks on the door and KC cuts the call and says, "Come in". Nandini, "Hey". KC, "Hey, had your reunion". Nandini, "Yeah they are waiting outside, do you want to meet them?". KC, "Why not but first tell me your purpose for coming". Nandini, "Oh so we have a theory behind President's missing. So, the President's car has about 3 cars in front and 3 behind escorting him, so they don't stop anywhere, as per the information we have, the only place the where the President can go missing was Sardar Patel Marg with the help of cameras covered in smog. So, whatever it is no car stopped in this entire journey, so the only possibility is President jumping out of the car. The reason is unknown but Driver is the only person in the car, so there might be some connection". KC, "Your theory could be correct and what I have with me right now is info from a bodyguard of the President, the president himself requested lone time and didn't want any of his men in the car, so as per his request there were no bodyguards in his car, but we got nothing from the driver so far.". Nandini, "and also we are assuming there might be some kind of threat or anything to the President's family which made him do that so I made Anupam and Akanksha monitor the calls, messages, emails everything of all his family members and also past calls and messages as well". KC, "Well fine, hope you make progress and we have the driver in our custody if you want to question him". Nandini, "Yeah". KC,"Let me take you guys to him".

KC, "Who is going to question him". Nandini, "Bhargava". Kc, "I would send a wild animal instead". Bhargava, "Am I not wild enough to be an animal". Kc, "You are worse". Nandini, "I will be monitoring his interrogation so calm down". Kc to Bhargava, "If you hurt him, I swear to God, I will kill you". Bhargava enters the room.

Driver: Sir, how many times will you question me?

Bhargava: Hey, are you ok?

Driver: No, I am not, I want to meet my family.

Bhargava: Did these guys feed you anything?

Driver: I don't care, I want to go, my family is waiting for me.

Bhargava is connected to a Bluetooth device so that he can be in contact with Nandini. Nandini receives information from Anupam that the Driver and his family have a flight to Dubai in an hour, Nandini shares this information with Bhargava. Chakith along with a few IIA officers takes the driver's family into custody.

Bhargava: So, you want to meet your family huh? Should I drop you at the airport so that you can fly to Dubai with your family, is that why you are so desperate to meet your family?

Driver: No no, I am not going anywhere.

Bhargava shows him a photograph of his family at the airport.

Bhargava receives another piece of information via Bluetooth device in his ear.

Bhargava: This is your family right, your son, wife, daughter. Cute. So, Vishal, that's your name right, or do you prefer me to call you with the name Jaffer alias Mohd. Jafferuddin Shaji.

Driver: Sir what are you talking about?

Bhargava: Your passport says that, is it your real name or just for the sake of your passport?

Driver: This is a piece of false information.

Bhargava: My friend from IIA had a small talk with your daughter's school teacher and she heard your daughter call you "abbu".

Meanwhile, Dinesh starts thinking, "Airport, Sardar Patel Marg, Rastrapathi Bhavan". Takes a paper and draws, "Let's assume Airport is point A and Rastrapathi Bhavan is point B and distance from A to Sardar Patel Marg is 'x' and distance from B to Sardar Patel Marg is also 'x' then the distance from Airport to Rastrapthi Bhavan is twice the x". Dinesh to KC, "Listen did you check all the CC cameras which passed to and from Sardar Patel Marg". KC, "Yes but President wasn't there in any of them". Dinesh, "then someone had to pick up the president right, if there is no President in any of those vehicles to and from Sardar Patel Marg at that time then the Kidnap was not done at Sardar Patel Marg". KC, "What are you talking?".

Bhargava: Are you a terrorist or what?

Driver: Sir, look at this rudraksha. I am not a terrorist.

Bhargava: Hara hara Mahadev. So where is the President?

Driver: I don't know.

Bhargava takes driver's hand, places it on the table and presses it so hard with his gun, and asks "Where is the President?".

Driver: I don't know.

Bhargava: Who is behind this?

Driver (cries in pain): I have no idea what you are talking about.

Meanwhile, Dinesh, "Sir it's a pattern. He diverted us. The kidnap didn't happen at Sardar Patel Marg, it happened in the Airport". Dinesh snatches the Bluetooth from Nandini and tells Bhargava, "Ask him whether is it Suraj Ali Khan behind this".

Bhargava: Suraj Ali Khan

Driver (stops crying): I swear I don't know who he is.

Bhargava: Now, I will broadcast the news that you leaked Suraj Ali Khan's name. And then his men will kill your family. Tell me the truth or else.

Driver(cries): I am Jaffer and I work for Suraj Ali Khan.

Bhargava: Where is the President now?

Driver: Hyderabad

Bhargava leaves the room goes to Dinesh and asks, "Who is Suraj Ali Khan?". Dinesh, "The one responsible for the massacre of a city, the one who killed hundreds of innocent people, the one who made our lives miserable, the one who won against IIA, the one whom we thought he is dead long back. The villain of 2020, Suraj Ali Khan alias Aditya".

Meanwhile, somewhere in India in a car with President tied in chains. The driver of the car, "Suraj bhai we reached Hyderabad". Aditya, "It's been 10 years since this city has seen the face of violence. I can hear the sound of peace, joy, it's irritating" pokes the president with a pin so hard he bleeds and President cries, Aditya, "This is the sound I like, don't be scared by seeing this burn on my cheek it's nothing compared to what you are going to witness (evil laugh) special song for you Mr. President, my favorites hope you like it". Plays the song, "Jeena Yahan Marna Yahan".

CHAPTER IX

Cat and Mouse

25 hours since the president went missing...

Bhargava was shocked after knowing Aditya is still alive. Nandini gets collars of Dinesh and asks, "You guys killed him right, in front of me, how did he get back alive". Dinesh, "I don't know". Bhargava, "We killed him, I am sure, I am 100% sure we killed him". KC, "What exactly happened that day?".

2020, it's been almost 3 days since the last attack took place. Akanksha accidentally left her system in the office and decided to collect it the next day. When she entered the office the next day, she found Dinesh doing something with the system. She asked, "Hey, what are you doing with my system?". Dinesh, "Just checking for the active bombs". She was like, fine. Everyone had come to the office to get some information and Dinesh was busy with the files and other information collection. Dinesh to Anupam, "Do you have the information on active terrorists now?". Anupam, "Yes". Anupam showed the list to Dinesh. Dinesh, "Fine, active agents undercover?". Anupam, "That's confidential". Dinesh, "Nothing confidential in IIA, we need to eliminate these guys without a mark on us, so that we can make our work easy with the help of contacting those guys". Nandini, "Fair point". Anupam gives the contacts to Dinesh and he started contacting them along with Akanksha, Nandini, and Bhargava. Suhaas rushed into the office and warned that there was a bomb blast in Apollo. Akanksha, "Dude the algorithm didn't give me any red dots, I am checking the history, no none, the information might be false. Are you sure? my algorithm never goes wrong". Suhaas, "it did, it's on news". Akanksha was in tears. Dinesh, "What's going on, what are we doing? Idiots. We are a pack of stupids. Fit for nothing". Nandini got a call from KC, "What's happening Nandini, 86 deaths single day". Nandini, "KC listen the algorithm went wrong". KC, "Prefer the old ways, I am talking with the PM for the arrangements, tight security in the public, I want no more life losses, understand". Nandini, "Yes sir, got it". Dinesh, "What now?". Nandini, "KC is coming to Hyderabad, he wants you to pick him up and he has something for you". Dinesh, "Fine I will pick him up". Dinesh left the office.

Bhargava, "This is growing bigger and bigger day by day 86 deaths and KC himself landing in Hyderabad". Nandini signals everyone to keep quiet and searches for bugs and found them, collected them, and put them in a silent room. Nandini, "We all were under observation". Bhargava, "What?". Anupam, "From when?". Akanksha, "No idea but today my brain started raising questions and I came to a conculsion". Chakith, "What exactly was happening?". Nandini, "Akanksha had given me a signal saying to send Dinesh out and search for bugs using morse code and also told me that it's red so I did what she said". Anupam, "Ok but why?". Akanksha, "You remember that day, the first bomb blast. Dinesh received a phone call, and after cutting there was a bomb blast right and Chakith told that the bombs are operated by a remote or a phone". Chakith, "Yes". Akanksha, "So, I ran a few tests on that phone and yes it's his phone which triggered the bomb". Anupam, "So you are saying that Dinesh was the one behind this?". Akanksha, "Who came up with the ideas on temples when Aditya gave us a hint?". Bhargava, "Me". Akanksha, "Were you sure about that?". Bhargava, "No was doubtful but Dinesh was sure. Wait". Akanksha, "Yes he diverted us, he delayed so that there will be a terrorist attack and once we involve in fighting the terrorists, he can plant the other bombs in other news channel offices". Chakith, "You are saying this now". Akanksha, "I was not sure until today, but I saw Dinesh handling my system, he inserted a bug that almost ate my code and I am reprogramming it, which is the reason why it couldn't detect the bomb". Nandini, "I know about Dinesh very well, I need proof to trust you". Bhargava, "Let us go to his house, we can find something right, related to this". Chakith, "It almost takes 2 hours for him to get back so let's go to his house quickly". Suhaas, "I will be here and I need Chakith so that he can assist if any bombs are detected".

Everyone went to Dinesh's house and were searching for some clues. Anupam heard a sound in the basement and informed Bhargava and Akanksha. They entered the basement and saw a person tied in a chair making noise. Bhargava pointed the gun at him. His face is covered with some cloth and had some blood on his feet. He was tortured for sure. Anupam removed the cloth on his face and to his surprise, it was Dinesh. Akanksha, "If this is Dinesh, who is he?". Dinesh, "Su...sura...". Anupam, "We are not able to hear you properly, first let's untie him". They untied him and with Bhargava's and Anupam's support, they brought him from the basement to the hall and another Dinesh was sitting on the couch eating popcorn. Another Dinesh on the couch washes his face with water and plucks out his skin on the face and reveals himself. It was Aditya.

Aditya, "Tough to live as a good guy, boring. Let me introduce myself, I am Aditya, first time right, it was nice to meet you guys". Akanksha texts Nandini, "We found Aditya". Nandini immediately gathered the entire force and started moving to the location. Aditya takes his gun in his hands, "Hey that guy is no traitor ok, he is a good guy, 2 days back I found his house and during his sleep, I injected him with a drug, tied him to a chair, and had fun with him. By fun I meant torture. It was fun playing another guy". Lights his cigarette and continues, "86 lives gone". Nandini has come with the force, no way left for him to go out. Aditya, "well played". Nandini, "Surrender". Aditya, "Seriously, dude I killed 86 people today and you ask me to surrender, if I was in your place I would directly shoot, this is not how justice works, what kind of system is this, Akanksha you reprogrammed your system right". Akanksha, "Yes". Aditya, "Good, by the way, if the entire force is here who will guard the public. There is a terrorist attack going on in Gandhi Hospital, Suhaas you are supposed to inform them right". Suhaas, "What?". Suhaas gets a call that there is a terrorist attack in Gandhi Hospital, and almost 60%of the patients, doctors, nurses who were treating patients were killed. Aditya, "by the way Akanksha your system had detected a bomb here, there is a red dot and we all are going to die here itself". Nandini, "everyone out". Aditya takes his phone out and then Dinesh takes Bhargava's gun and shot him, everyone ran away, and the bomb blasts. Suhaas gets a call, the additional forces were sent to Gandhi Hospital but the damage was high, almost 80% of them lost their lives and the remaining were injured. This was bigger than 26/11. This was a massacre. The failure of Team 2020. The team was dismissed. Bhargava was sent to Kashmir. Dinesh was posted to RAW. Akanksha and Anupam gave their resignation. Suhaas continued in the police department.

26 hours since the president went missing. Dinesh, "I remember I shot him that day. And then there was a bomb blast". KC, "So, after 10 years he is back, but how". Dinesh, "He always has a plan B. His strategies are extraordinary. Fucking mastermind. He calculates every possibility including the worst of the worst, so, no wonder how he survived the attack. He literally diverted the entire force to kill him just to make an attack successful, he gambled his life. So just imagine the extent he will go on other's life, the torture I went through, I can't even imagine what our President must be going through, we have to find him".

Nandini, "Jaffer has given the statement, Dinesh was right, the President was kidnapped in the Airport itself, and then Aditya became the President and jumped off the car and Jaffer closed the door and was on his way to the Rashtrapati Bhavan. The President was then taken to Hyderabad in a car". KC, "it takes almost a day to reach Hyderabad by car". Bhargava, "It's almost 26 hours since the president went missing, lets get a flight and go to Hyderabad". KC, "The checkpoints are alert and they are checking everything so don't worry we will get him". Dinesh, "No use, he will go through this". KC, "How?". Dinesh, "He is Aditya. He is planning something big, we have to reach Hyderabad quickly KC, now".

Hyderabad.

The person driving the car, "Suraj bhai there is a checkpoint ahead". Aditya, "Inject the president put him to sleep, don't stop move ahead". President went to sleep and the Police officer checked the car and found nothing, and asked for their ids. Aditya, "I am Aditya, he is my brother Arjun and these are my friends Ajay, Rahul, and the President of our gang Keshav". Officer, "fine you can go". Moving ahead Aditya, "we can change faces, we can be anyone, we can become Tom Cruise, President or Prime Minister. Next time let's kidnap the Chinese President, he is really irritating me". Driver, "Bhai we receive funds from China, we can't". Aditya, "Don't reveal our secrets to the President. Oh, sorry he is not President anymore, he is our friend Keshav". Song plays, “Kabhi kabhi mere dil mein khayal atha hain...”.

CHAPTER X

The President

Narration: Dinesh

28 hours since the president went missing...

10 years, it's been 10 bloody years since I stepped into this land. The city of Pearls, the land of Nizams, the royal city of the south, Hyderabad. Jaffer revealed that Aditya was the one who kidnapped the President and just entered Hyderabad. Our team along with KC just landed in Hyderabad. KC, "From where the hell did he enter the scene suddenly". Me to KC, "He didn't enter the scene, we are in the part of the scene he created". Nandini, "Seems like a perfect reunion". KC, "Suhaas is here". Finally, we meet Suhaas, he had put on weight and looked fat compared to the last time I met him. Suhaas, "Hello friends, I know now's not the perfect time for greetings, but how did he return". Chakith, "Even he wanted to be part of our reunion and make it special". Everyone turns to him and Anupam whispers to Chakith, "This was not the right time for dark humor, zip up your mouth". KC, "Now where?". Suhaas, "Secret, the Prime Minister is here in Hyderabad and wanted to meet you guys, so we are directly heading to meet him". KC, "Fine".

We all reached the NIA head office in Hyderabad and the Prime Minister is waiting to meet all of us. Finally, I saw the Prime Minister, it was the moment where you know it's like when a person whom you used to watch on TV is in front of you, what do you do, so I was in such a situation. We all sat and he started talking, "I heard that you guys are close to solving the case and found out that the President is in Hyderabad. So, I made sure that all the modes of transportation in Hyderabad are close for 24 hours". Anupam, "Sir please don't mind, but how?". PM with a smile replied, "Indian Politics make anything possible. The buses are on strike today, the reason you know is salary hikes but it's only you and I here who know the actual reason. It's been 45 years since I am in politics, and things will be managed. Similarly, the trains and airlines will be managed. Promise me that you find the president within 24 hours". Bhargava replied, "Promises, seriously, a politician is talking about promises here". KC, "shut up Bhargava". PM, "Calm down KC, look Bhargava I was a good man, now I am a politician, that good man had no power but this man you see has the supreme authority, that's the beauty of Indian politics, this system is power game and you are a small part of it, So, it's your responsibility to obey your higher authorities, (Shouts) so do as I say, understand. Any more questions?". KC, "I am sorry sir". PM, "Who is this guy, Aditya?". Nandini, "The man behind the 2020 attacks". PM, "That attack had a huge impact". I replied, “That attack has a huge impact on us too, that guy is a mad man, he can do anything, can become anyone, attack any place or beings, can kidnap anyone irrespective of how powerful they are, let it be an actor, sports person or a powerful politician, he is beyond power. The word danger is like a grain of sand to describe how he likes death music and he is competitive, he likes a tough opponent opposite to him, else he is such a psych that he helps his opponents to reach his standard and then defeats them. 10 years back we got nothing on him even though we had Akanksha's algorithm we were helpless he just played hide and seek. We didn't get any clues, but he gave us clues and he called us and gave us hints, such a humble gesture". PM, "So don't tell me that you guys are waiting for his call". The phone rings. Anupam lifts the phone and says, "Anonymous". Nandini, "Track It". Akanksha, "No use". Bhargava, "Answer the call". Me, "give it to me I will handle". Answered the call.

Aditya: Dhadkanon Mein Tere Geet Hain Mile Hue

Me: Kya Kahun Ke Sharm Se Hain Lub Sile Hue

Aditya: I missed this badly

Me: If you miss me, you can directly call me, no need of doing an adventure every ten years which grabs national attention.

Aditya: Adventures are fun. They entertain me, thrill me, and give me memorable moments with my school friends like you. It's fun. I also made new friends along with you. Nandini ma'am,

Anupam, Bhargava..

Me: I don't want to waste time talking shit. You obviously enjoy doing that but dude, let me be straight, Where in the seven hells is the president?

Aditya: In the 8th (laughs).

Me: It's not funny. What do you want?

Aditya: Ok, let's not waste time, I have more presidents to kidnap and cities to blast, very busy. Let's make a deal. Quick chalo fast.

Me: Deal? (Signals Anupam to make a note) what?

Aditya: M134 Minigun, Akanksha's algorithm has to be handed to me personally by you and most important Ali Azar Khan's release and leave him at the Pakistan border.

Me: I have to speak with the Government officials.

Aditya: The PM is with you, come on.

PM: The information about my location is confidential. How did he know?

Aditya: If I was in intelligence, I swear this country would be safest in the entire world.

Me: Agreed but let's come to the point. M134 is a dangerous weapon and how do you expect us to hand it out to a man like you, next Akanksha's algorithm, we can't risk national security, and next Ali Azar's release is impossible.

Aditya: Oh, so you guys don't want your president. Fine.

Me: The government doesn't agree.

Aditya: It's the Indian President. Obviously, the Indian government cares for the lives of VIPs, just look at the PM, and he will agree. The lives of VIPs are so dear to the PM, am I right, sir? ...

Me: I have to speak to him regarding this

PM: Give him what he wants

Aditya: Sounded like a politician. So bro when you start, you should have no phone, no watch, no gun nothing. Just wear the clothes of your choice and come to MGBS metro station, platform number 2, will meet you there, and wait till I come, have patience. Chalo bye.

(call disconnects)

Me, “How can he just cut the call?”. Nandini, “Things he asked for are very valuable”. PM, “Give him what he wants and get the President”. Nandini, “Sir but”. PM, “No more arguments, KC handle them, I will take a leave". PM left. Nandini, "KC, is the Prime Minister out of his mind". KC, "We have no option Nandini, send Dinesh with her Algorithm and M134". KC had arranged an M134 mini-gun, Akanksha gave her system and said, "there’s no backup, this is the only version I developed". Nandini gave me car keys and also a gun and said, "Fuck president, shoot him at sight, fuck rules, fuck the system". I replied, "Is this you? This is personal right. Keep the gun with you. Our job is to rescue the President. If he plans anything the team is ready, and we will handle it, first let’s get the President". Handed the gun to her and left the place. I went to the station, and the PM ordered the metro staff to allow the bags I was carrying and finally reached platform number 2 and was waiting for him to come, it was almost 2’o clock in the afternoon. Many trains have come and gone but he still didn’t come. It’s almost 10:30 PM. 43 hours since the President went missing and comes to the last train. The announcement says that this is the last train to Parade Grounds metro station. The doors opened. None in the train and then the song, “Jeena Yahan Marna Yahan...”. A man with a hoodie and black jeans got down from the last compartment. The lights started dimming and he started moving toward me and even I started moving toward him. He revealed himself and greeted, “Hello Dinesh, come on man give me a hug it’s been years we met”. I replied, “I remember the faces of every asshole I shot, but I still wonder how you escaped”. He replied, “Long story will discuss it in another meet”. I asked, “Where is the President?”. He replied, “Someone is in a hurry, first hand me those things I asked for and then you take the President along with you". Me, "Ali Azar just got released and we left him at the Pakistan border just now". Aditya, "Yeah just received the information. This system is so biased, is it. The people who have power, rule it. Your PM thought he was superior but now whom is he bound to”. Me, "A madman with no humanity, pity, respect, or any basic human qualities". I caught his hand and handcuffed him to the railing. Within seconds the police department and IIA were there and surrounded him. Aditya, "Good trap. Unexpected. But still, you didn't get your president". Me, "I don't want the president, I want you". He with disappointment, "Dramatic Indians, you guys want revenge. I expected a lot". I replied, "It's not revenge, it's justice". He clapped, "What a dialogue? Big fan, this country needs people like you but they deserve an asshole like me".

CHAPTER XI

The Massacre

Narration: Aditya

44 hours since the President went missing.

I am in a bloody police van. Ahh, these guys trapped me somehow and started taking me to the IIA head office. I was handcuffed and I have no idea what these people will do to me. They are taking me to the basement ok -2nd floor it is. And now I am in a room that has a table, 2 chairs, and handcuffs. So, they locked me in a chair and Dinesh sat opposite to me. The team has entered. I greeted them, "Hello everyone, hey tall guy, Chakith right, how do you diffuse such complicated bombs... really Akanksha, your algorithm was so cute, I wanted to cut it into tiny pieces, Anupam you gained weight, oops software, married, 2 kids, didn't invite me to your wedding, it would be a blast like not literally but a celebration kind of a blast, Bhargava cool down bro why so serious, learn to smile, is this how you welcome your guests?, Nandini how's your daughter you left her alone in your home with a baby sitter, what's her name?... ah Lakshmi, she stole some 3000 from your home, when you are back to Delhi remove her from the job, it's not fair ah, and Akanksha your son was crying since past 20 hours and your husband slapped him as well, take care of your son or else he will become like me one day, take care". Bhargava with his face red rushed to me with his pistol and pointed on my forehead and said, "I will kill you". I was scared, I swear I was scared, just covered my fear with a smile, that was the quote I read on Instagram, "cover your fears with a smile", so I just did it but it's not working over here, Dinesh controlled him, Nandini was like, "Dinesh will you kill him or shall I". Ok now someone or the other wants to kill me and then I started crying, "I am alone everyone wants to kill me, God why did you create me, ok fine shoot that bullet right come on, I die the President dies, wait the prime minister didn't call you, what the fuck". PM had called KC, "Where is the President?". KC, "On the way sir". I replied, "Hey cheating, this is cheating, you guys didn't find the President". Dinesh banged the table and replied, "If we didn't find the president, you guys kill this man, we blame it on you that you killed the president while we were giving what you guys asked for". I was shocked and asked, "You guys are clever, huh how did you plan all of these". Dinesh replied, "Taste of your own medicine and Azar Ali, we had to deal with Pakistan, so they returned him to us again. We just diverted you".

Me, “Mind games, mind games great, now let me continue the nation wants to know, the president is in Hyderabad, and a video of terrorists hitting the president with a crowbar is going viral in the media, is the hot news and is in almost all the news channel headlines of the world”. Suhaas rushed inside and I said, “Chill I already informed them, you are Suhaas right, you gained weight exercise don't be lazy”. PM calls KC again, "What's happening KC?". KC goes out and then I said, "See the PM wants the President back, you want me, you have to obey the Prime Minister, Prime Minister is in need of President, President is in our control and only person who can tell you where the President is, right now is me, so give me what I want". Dinesh, "Look I helped you when you were in need, when you were in your lowest, I was your friend". I interrupted him by saying, "Yes you saved me from the bullies because they showed me hell, now from whom will you save me, I am now the fking bully and you have to save the people from me, you have to not protect me but you have to protect from me, last time was not personal but this is personal, I am here just to meet you, and had come only for you, I am not the guy who was, introducing brand new me". Dinesh replied, "You are my friend, Aditya". I replied, "Yes, Aditya the guy who is just above the evils". Dinesh, "I am the other side of your coin, harnessing the light". Me, “But forgetting the fact that I am your darkness”. Dinesh stands and replies, “Oh you think darkness is your ally? You merely adopted the dark. I was born in it molded by it, the first light I saw in the darkness blinded me but showed me possibilities but unlike me, when I replied to light, you chose not to". In response I said, "I was in light but all it did was left me in the dark, I struggled a lot in the dark, I struggled until I became its ally. The light didn't deserve me but darkness is something of my type". Bhargava bangs the bench and with a loud voice, "Enough of your stupid childhood argument, just tell me where the fuck is the president". I replied, "M134, algorithm..". Bhargava presses his gun barrel at my forehead and tells, "Your life or M134". I laughed, "Life seriously, life is boring, kill me, kill me if you can, pull the trigger shoot me now, can you, can you?". Bhargava removes the gun. Dinesh sits and says, "Fine one last deal, you tell us where the president is and we give you what you want, a deal". I was convinced, "How can I trust you?". Dinesh, "Like you did in your 5th standard". I replied, "Fine he is in the 8th hell". Dinesh, "What?". I laughed and replied, "Musheerabad go and search". Everyone rushed out and there was a security guard left behind and the door was closed.

46 hours since the president went missing, finally the team found the president and they returned him to Delhi in a helicopter safely and celebrating. Then they reached the office but there was no office. The building was on fire and fire engines surrounded the building. Akanksha was on a stretcher. She is kind of alive but dead. So what happened? Did you guys expect a happy ending? Let's go back to where I was left out alone in my room. Remember never leave a madman alone in a room, especially with handcuffs.

44 hours since the president went missing,

I was bored, I needed a cigarette right now, and I called that man, "Heyy...do you have a cigarette". He has come near and kept the cigarette along with liter and a gun at an unreachable distance from my arms and said, "Choose carefully". I liked that guy, he made me angry and I started laughing, see when a madman like me, smiles it means he is done but when laughs it means, he wants more and I tried hard to unlock my cuffs took the gun and put a bullet in his head, son of a bitch. Took the liter and burned his body which triggered the fire alarm and cops were rushing, I just hid behind the door and when they entered, I stole a grenade from one of the officers removed the pin threw it inside and closed the door, and ran away towards the lift and there I found a cop with AK47 and he pointed his gun at me, long time hand to hand combat huh, I really enjoyed the fight and finally took his AK 47 along with his extra bullets and went upstairs to 1st floor. My cigarette is still unlighted and as the doors of the lift door opened, i threw a grenade and started firing giving no time for the cops, picked up a few guns from the dead cops and shot the remaining, before shooting them I asked one of the guards, "Tell me where M134 is, I will leave you". He pointed me to that M134 so I took it and rushed back to the lift. The doors closed now I am going to the 2nd floor. The cops are ready in the position to attack as soon as the door opens but surprise mother fuckers, it was M134, bullets started pouring and the cops standing against me started screaming for their lives, what a piece of pleasant music, wow. Music, wait a minute, cops here are injured not dead, "does anyone here has earphones?, I want some music". I found one and then killed everyone with music running old classic bollywood songs I prefer should kill the kakkars after this. Come on if you are wondering which song, you are not my fan, it's the "Jeena yahan marna yahan" remix. 3rd floor, forgot to light up the cigarette, ok let's do this after cleaning this floor, the door opened the music started Jeena yahan marna Yahan and now, I live, you die and you all are dead. Successfully cleaned the 3rd floor. So, after cleaning the 4th floor I found out that Akanksha and Anupam are on the last floor i.e 5th floor and now I need the algorithm and the bullets are done.

The doors of the lift opened and I am left with a lighter and a cigarette. I stepped out and was like, "Anupam, Akanksha, where were you?". Akanksha suddenly showed up with a gun. I said, "Oh dear look, what you have become, give me that gun or give me the algorithm", Akanksha, "I gave the algorithm to the boys, and they took it along with them". I replied, "You always keep your algorithm with you, don't you, even you didn't care to dedicate it after Hyderabad's massacre". Akanksha, "Algorithm is in my mind but the system in which the algorithm runs is not with me now". I was frustrated and kicked Akanksha, snatched the gun from her hand and threw it outside and started punching on her face, "Bitch give me the algorithm, you named your system algorithm just to confuse people, but I am not, where is it or else I will kill you, your son, your husband". Akanksha's face was like someone painted her with red and she was screaming in pain and finally said, "Anupam, it's with Anupam". I asked, "where is Anupam? Anupam, I know you are here where are you?, if you won't show up with the algorithm, I am goanna kill your friend your wife next and then your kids". Anupam shows up and says, "I have no algorithm". I caught her hair and dragged it and hung her such that her fall from the 5th floor of the building depends on her hair in my hand. Me to Anupam, "Say it or else she will die, Anupam come on, 10 seconds get the algorithm". 10 Anupam rushed to his cabin 9 8 7 6 5 3 2 1 and brought the algorithm but 10 seconds done so I lighted the hair in my hand with the lighter so that it burns the connection and the hair tears and she falls from the 5th floor and she fell and I had some part of her hair in my hand. Me, "See, you are late, learn to be punctual, and give me the algorithm". Anupam cries and I said, "Enough of mourning my friend, if not today then she has to die someday, right, learn to treat the dead with smile". Anupam takes the fire extinguisher and smashed my face that was a painful one. And then I attacked his feet for which he fell and took that fire extinguisher and hit him until he was used to that pain and stopped screaming, then I found a blunt knife, took it but something was missing, fine let me play the song, it's Jeena Yahan Marna Yahan but violin cover. Let me play violin with Anupam, so I put the knife on Anupam's neck and just followed the tune and played violin with knife and neck, and the best part was the tune was in perfect sync with me. I took the algorithm and went to the terrace the chopper landed and they are my terrorist friends, rich terrorist friends. So, after getting into the chopper we bombed the building and threw the algorithm in that fire before throwing the algorithm there were 4 red dots on it. My terrorist friend asked me, "Hey you didn't light the cigarette why? didn't you have a lighter". I replied, "I have, but smoking is injurious to health". I threw the cigarette in the fire and continued, "And also causes cancer".

Dinesh and the team found the President and they thought they won but they didn't know what I have done. They were celebrating the victory but after coming back what they found were burned bodies. And then I called him and said, "Dude I escaped and there are 4 bombs planted in India, nuclear, made in Russia, so all the best you have 5 days and the effect of the bomb wipes almost 2 cities so it will be 8 cities this time and I know you are feeling sad that you missed me in action so the CC camera footage is available i just sent you the video in telegram, have popcorn while watching it". Dinesh to Nandini, "This guy diverted us, he used President's kidnap as a diversion and planted four nuclear bombs in India, none noticed coz everyone was behind the President, now we have no techies, no algorithms nothing" Nandini, "What are we going to do then?". Dinesh, "Unfortunately they have to win once and we have to win million times and every time we win, every time a new problem starts, for every next one they grow stronger we become weaker but still we have to fight, after the end of every fight there arises a new problem, but in this case, the same problem continued".

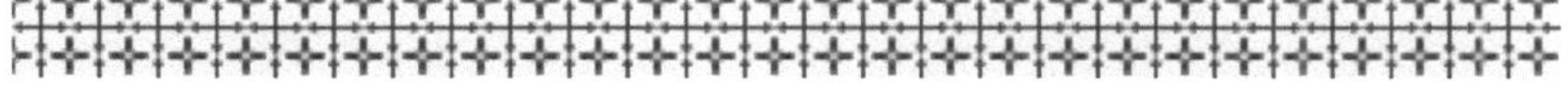

48 hours the president has been found. End of part 1
5 minutes since the bomb's activated...

..... TO BE CONTINUED

• • •

Somewhere in Russia, a man enters the President's cabin and whispers in his ear, "Sir our nuclear bombs went missing". President replied, "From when". That person, "Since 72 hours". 24 hours before the President went missing....

Printed by Libri Plureos GmbH in Hamburg,
Germany